Day of Violence

To Clem Winters and Doc Foran, as they rode out slowly west through the wide cattlelands, the name of the Texas Dusters was little more than a legend they had heard in the bigger towns along the trail. But it was soon obvious that to the men around the isolated township of Bitter Ridge it was more than a name, for these were the slickest band of cattle rustlers in the business.

As strangers in town, it was not long before Winters and Doc found themselves in real trouble, suspected of being in cahoots with the rustlers. When the showdown came they would have to prove themselves two of the fastest, straightest-shooting lawmen in the whole of the West.

Sudden death was the grim alternative.

Day of Violence

JOHN GLASBY

A Black Horse Western

ROBERT HALE · LONDON

© 1964, 2005 John Glasby
First hardcover edition 2005
Originally published in paperback as
Day of Violence by Chuck Adams

ISBN 0 7090 7692 4

Robert Hale Limited
Clerkenwell House
Clerkenwell Green
London EC1R 0HT

Typeset by
Derek Doyle & Associates, Shaw Heath.
Printed and bound in Great Britain by
Antony Rowe Limited, Wiltshire

CHAPTER ONE

TWIN BUTTES

Over to the east the sky was greying as Clem Winters came out of his room at the small hotel, went down into the yard at the back and stuck his head under the pump, scrubbing himself down vigorously before drying off with the coarse, heavy towel that hung on a nearby rail. It wanted an hour before dawn and the storm that had blown over the desert around the township of Twin Buttes still made itself felt in the chill wind that keened cold across the open yard, kicking up the white-grey dust into whirling shapes that stung his eyes as he dried his face.

There had been no rain with yesterday's storm, only the fierce wind which had blown up suddenly and without warning around noon, lifting the arid, alkali dust from the stretching desert, pitching it high into the air to form a solid curtain of irritating grains, sending it hurtling down on to the winding trail, catching Doc Foran and himself in the open. There had been no shelter for miles as they had put their mounts to a gallop, trying to run before it. They had finally ridden into this small town an hour before sundown, although by that time, with the storm at its height, the sky had been blotted out completely by the dust cloud and there had been no sign of the sun.

He pushed his fingers through his wet hair, then shook his head sharply, buttoning his shirt as the wind still cut cold against his flesh. Tall and rangy, the shirt strained across his shoulders as he moved, and his face was burned a deep brown by long exposure to the sun, his eyes a slatey-grey, far-seeing and direct in their gaze.

Doc Foran cause out of the hotel a moment later, looked up at the sky with a shrewdly appraising glance, then across at his partner.

'How long you figuring on staying around these parts, Clem?'

'Hard to say. Until we pick up some information, I guess.'

Doc worked the handle of the pump for a moment. 'This seems to me to be one hell of a town, Clem. If Goudie is around here any place, I reckon Twin Buttes is as good a town as any along the trail where he can stop running. There'll be more of his kind here. This part of the territory has got a reputation for offering shelter to the wild bunch.'

'We know he started out over the desert back a piece,' pointed out Clem. 'And if he didn't stop here, he'll have to keep on running clean over the desert and out to the mountains. Ain't likely he'll do that. Not if he suspects we're as close as this on his trail.'

'That desert out there,' said Doc, towelling himself down, 'is close on fifty miles across and half as broad. How do you figure on covering all of that, looking for a killer like Goudie?'

Clem nodded. 'Pretty soon he's going to get tired of all this running. He's either going to bump into some of his own kind and turn and fight, or he'll do that even if he's still alone. A man has only a certain amount of steam in him. When that's gone, all used up, he has to stop.'

He searched for his tobacco, rolled a smoke, struck and cupped a match to his face after letting the sulphur tip burn off. He breathed deeply on the cigarette and blew out smoke.

To the east, the sky was now appreciably brighter than before and there was red mingled with the grey as the sun began to come up. There were large clear patches of sky and the clouds were clearing quickly although the smell of dust still lay thick in the air. Clem rubbed absently at his cheek where the irritating grains of dust were still embedded deeply in his flesh.

Doc said: 'You reckon that he might even make a play in town?'

'Maybe. If he does, we'll be ready for him. I figure we'd better split once we've eaten. We'll talk back here at the hotel tonight.'

'Move easy in town,' said Doc, pausing in the doorway, his hat balanced on his iron-grey hair. 'I've got the feeling that they look twice at all strangers riding into town. I don't reckon they'd fancy a couple of lawmen in their midst.'

'You're darned right.' Clem gave a tight grin, went up to his room and buckled on the gunbelt, before coming downstairs into the small dining-room for breakfast. Through the window near the table, it was possible to look out along most of the length of the main street of the town. On the face of it, the place seemed little different from countless other towns they had ridden through. There were two general stores sitting side by side on the other side of the street and then the barber's shop, crushed up against the side of the sheriffs office and just beyond, the town newspaper, with faded gold lettering across the glass of the wide window.

He ate heartily, washed the food down with hot coffee, then got to his feet, looking down at Doc. 'See you tonight,' he said casually and strolled out of the room.

Eyes followed him as he stepped out of the hotel on to the boardwalk, then went down the one step into the dusty street. Where to begin? he wondered. There were so many places a man could hide in a town like this; and it was just possible that Goudie had not stopped, but had ridden through, counting on the storm to hold them back.

Acting on impulse, he walked over to the sheriff's office, pushed open the door, and stepped inside. The sheriff was seated at the long desk, his legs up, crossed easily at the knee. He eyed Clem over them, then lowered them to the floor and sat back in his chair. He was a short man, broad, hard, with clear blue eyes that seemed to bore right into a man, as if looking down into his very soul.

'You the sheriff here?' asked Clem.

The man nodded, jerked a thumb in the direction of the other chair. 'That's right, the name's Thorpe. You just riding through?'

Clem lowered himself into the chair, then shook his head. 'I'm looking for somebody, Sheriff. I guessed he might head this way, was following his trail across the desert yesterday when the storm broke. I lost him then, but I figure this is the only place he could come.'

Thorpe lifted the thick black brows. 'There's no other town within fifty miles of Twin Buttes,' he agreed. 'But I ain't heard on no stranger riding in, except for the man who came with you.' His eyes were fixed on Clem's face and there was a look of almost amused intent in them, as if he anticipated that the fact he knew of Doc's presence in town might come as a surprise to Clem. If he did, then he was disappointed.

Clem showed no surprise, except for the slight narrowing of his eyes. He kept his gaze fixed on the sheriff.

'This man Goudie a friend of yours?' inquired Thorpe. He eyed Clem seriously.

8

'Not exactly. He's wanted for murder and armed robbery down in Tucson.'

A sharp look came into the other's eyes at that. Clem felt a little warning bell ringing in his mind. In a town like this, about which he knew nothing, it was perhaps not wise to trust anybody, even the sheriff himself until one was absolutely sure.

Thorpe said: 'That being so, Mister, what's your interest in him? Unless you're a Ranger. Are you?' The way he said it made the words sound flat and ugly things.

Clem shook his head slowly, noticed the speculative gleam in the sheriffs eyes. 'Don't really like to spread the nature of my job around, Sheriff,' he said cautiously. 'Some folks don't like men such as me.'

He saw the momentary expression of distaste on Thorpe's face, knew the other was thinking along the lines he wanted him to. 'A bounty hunter.'

'Sure – and why not? Somebody has to go out and bring 'em in – dead or alive. Why not pay us for risking our necks in this way?'

As far as the town was concerned, this was as good a guise as any for him. Generally, bounty hunters were held in contempt by most people, but if what he expected about this town was anywhere near the truth, he might get more information this way than if it were known that he was a lawman

'I'd be careful what you say around town,' murmured the other softly. 'Folk here might not take too kindly to a man like yourself. On occasion, this is a real lawless town, I'll admit that. We try to keep some form of law and order here but we're isolated and this is the last outpost before the run across the desert and out to Bitter Ridge.'

'But you haven't any idea whether this man is here in town?'

Thorpe shook his head. 'If he is and I find him first, I'll

bring him in myself.' He rummaged in the drawer of the desk, then looked up. 'No posters here about any man called Goudie. You sure that's his name?'

'It's the one I know him by.'

The sheriff pondered on that for a moment, staring past Clem. Then he said deliberately: 'I'm not making it an order to take things easy in this town. I suppose you've got a reason for doing this job, although I can't say that, as a lawman, I approve of it; but so far, you've done nothing against the law. But for your own safety, don't push folk too far here in Twin Buttes. There's a real big difference between pushing a man just far enough and pushing him over the line.

'You'll find that they don't like strangers here, particularly those who have the smell of a bounty hunter about them.' His glance dropped to the twin guns at Clem's waist. 'You look to me like a fella who knows how to use those guns,' he said gently, 'but life can be pretty cheap here.'

'Aren't you supposed to be the law in the town?'

'Sure.' Thorpe nodded, sharpness edging his tone. 'Only I ain't such a fool as to think I can fight these men single-handed and there aren't too many men I can trust in town to swear in as a posse, even if I did decide to go out after them.'

'I see your point.' Clem nodded, then got to his feet. 'Thanks for the warning, Sheriff. I'll bear it in mind. If I do find the man I'm looking for, I'll bring him back here for you.'

'Do that.' Thorpe gave a quick nod, put his feet back up on to the desk and looked dreamily out of the window nearby on to the street. He seemed to have completely forgotten Clem's presence there.

Outside, Clem blinked against the harsh glare of sunlight. He had not realized how dim it had been in the sheriff's office. He lit a smoke, appraised the street from one end to the other. Twin Buttes swarmed with traffic now. A wagon train had moved in to buy stores before taking the trail. Cattle drovers drifted among the wagons and prairie schooners. Gamblers in their jim-swinger coats mingled with a few Indians who had moved into this frontier town from the hills. Everywhere, there were dogs and horses, both following in the wake of man across a vast continent.

He let his gaze wander over the stores on the opposite side of the street, a thought forming in his mind. If Goudie had ridden into Twin Buttes some time during the previous day, then he might need stores if he intended moving out as soon as possible, heading west across the alkali desert towards the mountains. There was a tension in his manner as he crushed the smoke out in the dust with his heel and walked over to one of the stores. The place was full of women in their poke bonnets, women from the wagon train outside in the street. He waited patiently while they made their purchases and then went up to the long counter. The man at the back of it looked up. His face was filmed with sweat as he totted up the list of figures on the pad in front of him.

'You want some stores, mister?' he asked hoarsely. Clem shook his head. 'Just some information,' he said quietly. 'I'm looking for a man who may have ridden through the town yesterday. If he did come in, then he's either still here or he's headed west. In that case, he'd need supplies to get him across the desert.'

'And you reckon he may have come here.' The other cocked his head on one side and fixed beady eyes on Clem, lips pursed.

'He may have.' Clem took the folded poster from his shirt pocket and spread it out flat on the counter in front of the other. 'This is the man I'm looking for. Have you seen him?'

11

He thought he saw a sudden gleam in the other's eye as the man stared down at the poster, but it was gone a second later and when the man looked up at him once again, it was gone, wiped away and there was only a set, blank expression. He shook his head. 'Never seen him, mister. Sorry. Why're you looking for him, anyway?'

'He's wanted in Tucson for murder and armed robbery,' said Clem simply.

'You a lawman?'

'Nope. But I've been trailin' him for days now. Lost him in the desert during that storm yesterday.'

'Well, I ain't seen him. He's never been in here for supplies.'

'You're sure?'

'Course I'm sure. Do you think I'd forget a face like that? Yesterday, you say?' He shook his head emphatically. 'Nobody here that looked like that.'

Clem replaced the poster in his pocket. If you do see him, would you get in touch with me at the hotel, or Sheriff Thorpe?'

'Sure, sure.' It was clear that the other was anxious that Clem should leave and that this conversation should be terminated. Nodding, Clem turned and walked out. He didn't doubt that the other knew far more than he was telling, that Goudie had been in the store, had picked up supplies. That posed the problem. It suggested he had ridden out shortly after arriving and that meant he could be halfway across the desert now, headed in the direction of the next town – Bitter Ridge. It was unlikely that he would head south, back to Tucson, or east. West was the way he would go and every minute Doc and he remained in Twin Buttes, meant that Goudie was putting more miles between himself and them.

Throughout the afternoon he checked with the livery stables and other stores, but everywhere, the answers were

12

the same. No one had seen a man of that description the previous day. Most of the people were speaking the truth, Clem felt sure of that. But there were others who were lying. He did not know the reason why they lied. There seemed no reason why they should want to protect, to shield, this cold-blooded killer. Yet they persistently disclaimed all knowledge of him when it was obvious that they knew something.

That evening, at the hotel, he went in to supper, sat down at the small table near the window and waited for Doc Foran. The other came in fifteen minutes later, glanced across the room, saw him, and walked slowly over. His face bore a serious look as he sat down opposite Clem.

'Well?' Doc asked tightly, 'Did you find out anything about Goudie?'

'Only that we figured right. He's been here but I doubt if he still is in town. There are several folk lying to shield him for some reason. Could be that they're scared. There's a lawless element in this town that might make it hard on them if they learned they'd talked to us about him.'

Doc nodded, gave his order to the bartender, then leaned forward with his arms on the table. 'I got the same feeling. He was over at the far livery stable on the edge of town, saw his mount there.'

'Then that means he's still in town?' Clem glanced up, interested and something else showing at the back of his eyes.

Doc shook his head. 'Afraid not, Clem. I asked the hand about the horse. Admitted that the owner rode in yesterday. but wouldn't identify him from the poster. Said the fella who brought him in, traded him for another and rode out immediately afterward.'

'Then he must be out in the desert somewhere, proba- bly heading west as fast as he can push that horse.' Clem chewed slowly on his food. He lifted his head, then swung his gaze back across the room. At one of the tables on the far side, a man sat watching him and there was more than a casual interest in the other's level gaze. He caught Clem's glance and held it, as direct as his was now. He was a man like other men they had met on the trail, and there was the white dust of the desert on his shirt, and a black growth of stubble on his chin. Evidently he had just ridden in from the trail. He continued to watch Clem and he thought he saw the break of deeper interest in the man's eyes as he finally turned away and spoke to the bartender, who went over to him.

Switching his gaze back to Doc, he saw the other eyeing him curiously. 'Somethin' wrong, Clem. You look as though you've seen a ghost.'

'I'm not sure. There's a *hombre* at one of the tables back there who seems to be mighty interested in us. I'm trying to recall ever having seen him before, but his face ain't familiar.' He shrugged, glanced up again, but saw to his surprise that the chair at the table was empty and the bartender was moving back to the bar. Glancing aside swiftly, Clem noticed that the door of the dining-room was just closing, as if someone had left in a hurry.

'You're sure it wasn't Goudie?'

'Positive. But he certainly seemed to reckon he knew us. Could be that the sheriff had sent him to keep an eye on us.'

'Why should he do that?' Doc inquired.

Clem gave a tight grin. 'I had a word with Sheriff Thorpe. He wasn't too keen on anybody asking questions around town. Figured it might be dangerous for us, even admitted that there could be trouble and he didn't have the men to deal with it if there was.'

'That sounds like the kind of town I had figured this morning.' Doc finished his food and drained the coffee at

14

his elbow. 'I reckon we'll get nothing out of the people here. We'd be better saddling up and riding west at dawn. See if we can't pick up his trail in the desert. After all, except for the wagon trains, there won't be many people use that trail.'

'Perhaps you're right, Doc.'

'Dammit, Clem, I know I'm right' The other sounded adamant. 'We're wastin' precious time here.'

Leaving the dining-room, they made their way through the small lobby and up the stairs to their rooms. As they approached the end of the corridor, one of the doors opened and a man stepped out into the passage. Clem glanced up sharply, then recognized him as the man who had shown so much interested curiosity back in the dining-room, the man who had disappeared shortly after Clem had turned his gaze back on him.

The man came up to them in the dim light from the two lamps at either end of the passage, bent towards Clem. 'Match?' he asked softly. There was a smoke in his mouth, unlit.

'Sure.' Clem brought out a match, struck and held it out to the other. The man drew deeply on the cigarette, then flicked a quick, almost nervous, glance along the passage at Clem's back, sweeping it thoroughly with his gaze. Then he said harshly: 'I hear you've been asking about a man who rode through here yesterday. I reckon I can tell you something about him. Can we talk in your room. It might not be too healthy out here where we can be seen.'

Clem nodded quickly, threw a swift look at Doc, then turned the key in the door of his room and motioned the other inside. Once Doc had passed through, he closed the door softly and locked it. Then he went over to the window and pulled the heavy curtain across it, shutting off all view from the street.

'You've got some information on this man we're lookin' for?' he asked, turning back. The other sank down into one of the chairs, nodded slowly. Now that he could see him clearly for the first time, Clem saw that he was obviously one of the storekeepers in the town. Short in stature, broadly built, once muscled but now going to fat, he seemed nervous and ill at ease.

'I think so. If it's the same man. You still got that picture of him I could take a look at?'

'Sure.' Clem dug it out of his pocket, handed the poster to the other. The man took it, spread it out on his knees with fingers that trembled a little. Then he nodded. 'That's him all right. Rode in shortly before noon yesterday, stopped at my place to buy a new Colt and some shells. Said he would be riding out of town as soon as he'd eaten, that he was heading west.'

Doc gave Clem a sharp glance, then said: 'We understand that there's nothing but desert to the west of Twin Buttes, until you get to Bitter Ridge and that's the best part of fifty miles away. Along ride through bad country. Did he say why he was heading that way?'

'Not exactly.' The man handed the poster back to Clem. He sat with his hands resting on his knees, and every now and again he would throw a quick look in the direction of the curtained window, as if expecting to see someone twitch the curtains back and step through with a gun. He pulled hard on the cigarette until the end glowed red, then blew the smoke out in front of his face. 'If anybody in town knows that I've been here talking to you like this, it'll mean trouble.'

'No reason why anybody should know anything. Just tell us all that you know and we'll be riding out first thing in the morning. Like as not, you'll never see either of us again.'

The man pondered on that for a long moment, then

16

nodded. 'He seemed anxious to get some information about the Texas Dusters, said there might be a job for him with them if he could only link up with them. Figured they had to have their hideout somewhere in the hills along the edge of the desert.'

'The Texas Dusters?' Clem looked at him, brows lifted into an interrogatory line.

The man gave a quick nod. 'Reckon you must be strangers in these parts if you never heard of them. They're the slickest bunch of rustlers this side of the Rio Grande. Operate around Bitter Ridge, where most of the big spreads are. They say they've taken nearly thirty thousand head of cattle during the past couple of years and they've never been caught.'

'And if Goudie is smart, he'll get himself in with them. Then we'll have the devil's own job trying to get him out of those hills.'

Doc Forman said: 'You know anything about these rustlers, mister? Could be that if we knew who to look for we might—'

'Nobody knows anythin' about them,' said the storekeeper. 'They don't operate around here. We only hear about them whenever anybody from Bitter Ridge rides into town. They're something of a legend on the other side of the desert.' He sat forward on the edge of his chair and looked up with a faint expression of surprise on his face. 'Say, you two ain't thinking of setting yourselves up against them, are you?'

'Depends,' said Clem coolly. If this man does get in with them, then we shall have to go against them.'

The other got to his feet, looked from one man to the other in slight bewilderment. 'I hope you know what you're up against,' he said thinly. 'Seems the law ain't able to do anything. Don't see how two men can stop them when the posses from Bitter Ridge can't find any sign of 'em.'

He walked to the door, turned the key, opened it, and stepped out into the passage, threw a swift glance along it in both directions. Then he looked back for a moment. 'Don't forget,' he said hoarsely, 'I ain't told you anything.'

'We'll remember,' Clem told him. He closed the door behind the other, then moved back into the room, sat down and rolled himself a smoke. 'Do you think he was telling the truth?'

'I reckon so,' Doc nodded. 'Ain't no reason why he should lie to us. He was plumb scared all the time he was talking. If he's right, it sure looks bad. By himself, out there in the desert, we'd have a good chance of trailing him. But if he joins in with a cattle rustling outfit, we don't stand much of a chance.'

'It's the only lead we've got,' said Clem bitterly. 'We've come this far, I reckon we can go a little further.'

Before the dawn came they were out of town, on to the rough grass, turning westward immediately, giving their mounts their heads, so that they moved with a slow, but mile-eating lope. It was very quiet all around them. Directly ahead, the trail wound between the tall, rising mounds of smooth rock, the twin buttes which gave the small town its name. Beyond them, lay the desert proper. As they rode, the only sound in their ears was the fine whistle and rustle of the wind in the long coarse grass that grew thickly along both sides of the trail, and the steady beat of the horses' hoofs on the hard-packed earth of the trail.

On a low rise of land a mile west of the town, they paused, reined their mounts and looked back behind them. In the dim light, with the thin slice of yellow moon low against the horizon, and the faint greyness of the coming dawn at the back of the houses and buildings, Twin Buttes still seemed to be asleep. Clem sat easily in the saddle, permitted himself to think of Goudie, a born killer who had led a gang of bandits that had robbed seven stages in five months around Tucson. There was a price of three thousand dollars on the man's head and Doc and he had been given the job of running him down and bringing him back to Tucson to stand trial for his crimes. Had it not been for that freak storm which had blown up with an unprecedented fury two days earlier, when they had been close on his heels on the trail, they might have caught up with him before he had reached Twin Buttes, and then it would have been a very different story. As it was, their task had now been made a hundred times more difficult because of that unforeseen delay.

'It's going to be a long ride and a hot day.' Doc glanced up at the brightening heavens in the east where the stars were beginning to dim before the dawn. 'Reckon we'd better make tracks before the heat comes. It ain't going to be nice out there in the desert.'

'Somehow, I figured there might be a posse out on our tail once the sheriff found out we'd left town.'

Doc lifted his brows. 'Now why in tarnation should he do that?'

'Just a hunch. I got the feeling he wasn't too keen on us tracking down Goudie. It's a lawless town back there and if you want to stay in office as sheriff, you've either got to run every gunslinger out of town, or go in with them. I reckon Sheriff Thorpe went in with 'em. If that's the case, and they hear we're trailing this man Goudie down, the lawless element in town could have prevailed on him to get a posse out after us, before we can reach Goudie.'

'A case of thieves' honour.' Doc gave a quick, down nod of his head. He squinted back along the trail. 'No sign of anybody coming yet,' he remarked.

They wheeled their mounts and rode quickly along the dusty trail towards the buttes. To their right and left the land lay in a sea of rolling grass, almost as far as the eye could see, and in the distance to their right, he could see the black mass of cattle grazing on the low hills. Rich hunting grounds for men like the Texas Dusters, he reflected; and yet according to the gunsmith back in town, they never operated in this area.

Through the rising stone of the buttes where it lifted sheer on either side of the trail, almost blotting out the sky for them. Then they were through and the vista that opened up in front of them was one of complete change. The land was flat so that it was possible to make out the hazy outline of the mountains on the western skyline at least fifty miles away. The sunlight was just beginning to touch the peaks in the far distance with a rose flush, so that they stood out from the desert which lay still in shadow. Behind them, the sun was not yet above the horizon and the air was still cool on their faces.

The coolness lifted Clem up. From here on, it was desert, but the coldness of night still lay on it and there was no indication of the terrible, searing heat which would come with the morning.

The sun came up, rose into the zenith, throwing short shadows around them. By now, they were well into the desert and there were no trails here on the shifting alkali. All a man could do was ride for the distant mountains, keep them directly ahead of him and hope that he encountered one of the few waterholes along the route.

Doc lifted his wide-brimmed hat and wiped the sweat band with his bandanna, gave a brief sigh. 'Sure gets hot out here in the middle of all this. Can't figure any man who would come riding out here unless he had to.'

'Goudie has a reason,' Clem reminded him. He pushed his vision through the shimmering heat haze that danced tantalizingly all about them. Dust devils whirled and cavorted along the low ridges. A terrible and inhospitable

20

land this, where nothing ever grew, where nothing would ever grow. No miracle was going to make this country bloom, thought Clem dispiritedly. He let his narrowed gaze wander in every direction. There was, of course, always the possibility that Goudie had not travelled quite as far as they had expected; there were places here, even in this rolling flatness, where a man could crouch behind one of the long, low ridges and cut them down with well-aimed shots from a Winchester, long before they got within range of him with the Colts.

The first waterhole they came across was dry, little more than a shallow depression in the ground, flat stones on the bottom, gleaming a bleached white in the intense sunglare. The slight course that wound up to it from the north looked as if no water had flowed along it for many years. Doc gave it a shrewd glance, then shrugged. 'There's been a drought here for some time by the look of that, Clem. We may find that every hole is like this.'

'We got plenty of water to see us across if no storm blows up.'

'I'm wondering about Goudie. Did he take plenty of water with him?'

'He must have. He's no fool, otherwise he'd never have got as far as this and a man doesn't head out into the desertlands without taking plenty of water with him.'

Doc Foran wiped the sweat from his forehead, where it dripped into his eyes, and nodded slowly. Around them, the desert was one vast cauldron where the heat was refracted from white alkali and rocks in one dazzling glare that hurt the eyes to look at it, even forced its way through closed lids as a dark red glare that burned into the brain. A man would go blind out here if he had to stay for any length of time.

Gradually, the sun began to move along its slow, downward dip towards the west, but the heat head continued, a

21

vast pressure over the world, heavy and oppressive. They rode slowly now, their mounts picking their way carefully over the burning heat of the alkali, the irritating and caustic dust working its way into their hoofs. It was blazing hot now, the sun moving around until it began to face them and there was no way of escaping the terrible glare. They struck another wide, sandy bed that had once been filled with water., flowing down from the hills far to the north. Now there was only the white-grey of the punished earth, with the heat still making a thin, barely-seen turbulence all around them.

They made camp that night at the first waterhole they had seen which was not dried up. Here there was a thin trickle of muddy water that flowed over the sandy stream bed. Where the watercourse looped in a wide, curving sweep, they tethered the horses and spread out their blankets on the hard floor of the desert.

There was no fuel for a fire and after they had eaten cold jerked beef, washed down with the water from their canteens, they rolled themselves in their blankets. The sun had dropped out of sight behind the tall, undulating line of mountain peaks in the far distance and as the deep blackness of the desert night settled over the world, blotting out every last vestige of colour in the arch of the heavens, the heat began to dissipate rapidly and soon the cold began to take its place, settling deep into their bones as they pulled their bedrolls more tightly about their bodies.

As he lay in the blankets, Clem could hear the horses moving around, restless in the desert, uneasy in that alien country. He felt the continual itch of the alkali grains where they had worked their way into the folds of his skin, mingling with the sweat, abrasive and irritating.

He turned slightly on the ground, aware of the brilliance of the stars over his head, standing out like gems against the black velvet of the sky, seemingly so low and close that he had only to lift his hand to be able to touch them. Half-anhour later the moon came up, thin and pale, and the cold light that touched the desert was one which never had had any warmth in it and made him feel colder than before.

Turning his mind to Goudie, he tried to put himself in the other's place, tried to figure out what the killer would do, knowing that there were two lawmen very close on his trail, knowing too that they would never give up until either they or he were dead. It seemed reasonable to suppose that once he hit the desert trail he would keep on riding until he had crossed the desert and could lose himself somewhere on the other side.

Thinking of that, he began to wonder about the Texas Dusters. They sounded to be just the kind of outfit that Goudie would try for, if he ever managed to meet up with them. A gunman and a born killer, he could soon establish a place for himself with an outfit such as that; and once he did so, it was not going to be easy to pry him loose from it.

He heard Doc move, a short distance away and a moment later, the other's voice drifted across to him out of the cold darkness. 'Can't you sleep either, Clem?'

'Nope. Too much on my mind, I guess.'

'Still thinking about Goudie?'

'A bit,' Clem admitted. 'I'm trying to figure out what I would do if I was in his place, with a couple of lawmen after me.'

'And what do you figure you would do?'

'I reckon I'd try to join that outfit who's rustling all of the cattle on the other side of the desert.'

'Makes sense, I reckon. But you'd have to find 'em first and from what I gathered back in Twin Buttes, that ain't so easily done. Seems the law can't trail 'em to their hideout. What chance do you reckon Goudie has?'

'It's somethin' we've got to consider,' said Clem musingly.

Doc said something softly under his breath, then uttered a sharp hiss of warning. One of the nearby horses snickered quietly. It was only a soft sound but it carried easily and Clem felt a warning tightness in his mind. Very slowly and cautiously, he lifted himself up on one elbow and peered off into the clinging darkness that lay about them, eyes and ears straining to pick out the slightest movement and the faintest sound. He knew that his horse's hearing was far better than his own under these conditions and he had learned to trust the judgement of the big gelding. There was someone or something out there and the horse had detected it. A coyote? One of the scavengers of the desert, attracted by their presence there, possibly coming down to the waterhole to drink.

Carefully, taking no chances, his right hand reached out for the gunbelt lying close beside him and the heavy Colt made only the faintest whisper of sound as he slid it from leather and held it balanced carefully in the palm of his right hand, fingers curling around it, forefinger in the trigger guard.

There was a faint light over the desert and gradually, as his eyes became adjusted to it, he was able to make out the contours of the ground around them, the rising humps of the ridges that moved almost due east and west, paralleling each other. It was almost a minute later when he picked out the first, faint rumour of someone moving around in the desert not very far away, a quiet, stealthy movement which could only just be picked out above the great stillness of the desert.

Doc had heard it too, for a second later, he slipped from his blankets, motioned to Clem, then slithered out of sight along the side of the watercourse, the faint moonlight glinting off the metal of the gun he held in his right hand. The horse snickered again, more loudly this time. Clem felt his trail-tautened nerves draw tight, his ears attuned to the sounds around him, ignoring those that meant nothing, waiting to pick out the movements of the man who came edging in towards the camp. Carefully, slowly, he eased out of his own blankets. There was no sign of where Doc had gone but he guessed he was not far away. There was one thing about Doc, whenever he wanted to, he could move through country as silent as a Cheyenne brave, unseen and unheard.

The sharp bark of the rifle echoed over the desert a split second after the bullet had kicked up sand within a foot of Clem's position. He threw himself down on to his face, slithered forward and rolled to one side, away from the blankets that made a dark shadow on the ground, too easily seen from a distance. Another shot, but this time the bullet struck the ground yards away and he guessed that the drygulcher had lost him in the darkness, taken by surprise by his sudden move.

Swiftly, he loosed off a couple of shots along the side of the ridge that stretched away to the west. Neither bullet hit its mark, but he knew it would keep the bushwhacker busy while Doc worked his way around him, took him from the rear. He fired a third shot, then flattened himself to the ground as a slug hummed viciously close to his head. He had given away his position, and the drygulcher had spotted the muzzle flash of his gun. There was certainly nothing wrong with the other's aim, whoever he was.

Another shot and then there was answering fire from the edge of the ridge. From where he lay, Clem could just make out the faint shadow of Doc Foran as he fired at the man who had drygulched them. He emptied his gun in the direction of the other, pause& to reload the spent chambers. Before he could do so there was a brief lull in the rifle fire and then the sound of a horse galloping off into the distance, the hoofbeats muffled a little by the alkali.

Pushing himself to his feet, Clem ran towards where Doc lay, came up to him a few moments later and stood looking off into the darkness after the retreating man. Doc turned sharply, caught Clem by the arm to hurry him back to the camp.

'If we saddle up we might be able to catch him,' he said hoarsely.

Clem shook his head. 'Not a chance. He's got too good a head start on us. We'd never be able to follow him in this darkness. Let him go. There's no doubt who it was.'

'You reckon it was Goudie?' The other looked at him with his head cocked a little on one side.

'Of course it was. Couldn't have been anybody else. No one else would have opened fire on us like that, sneaking up out of the darkness and trying to take us while we were asleep.'

'Yeah, I guess you're right.' Doc holstered his gun reluctantly, paused for a moment on top of the ridge, staring off to the west, as if trying to push his sight further into the pale wash of yellow moonlight that lay over everything, to pick out the shape of the man riding swiftly into the distance. Then he uttered a heavy sigh and turned. 'We may be able to pick up his trail in the morning.' he said quietly. If there isn't any storm through the night his mount will have left good tracks in the alkali.'

The next morning, they ate a quick meal, then saddled up, tightening the cinches before climbing into the saddle. Fifty yards along the bottom of the ridge, they located the tracks of the rider who had attempted to kill them the previous night. They led off in a westerly direction for a mile or so and then swung sharply to the south as if the rider had suddenly changed his mind and decided to go off in a totally different direction.

'What do you make of that Clem?' asked Doc, sitting easily in the saddle and pointing to the trail.

'Could be that he figured we might decide to follow him and he's laying a false trail for us.'

'That's what I think,' agreed the other wisely. 'He wasted precious time last night coming back after us as he did and somehow, he has to make up the time he lost.'

'So he leads us on a detour to the south, while at this very minute, he's heading west. There's no place south of here he could go. Only the hills down there and then more desert.'

'Then the advantage is still with us.' Doc Foran wheeled his mount, deliberately ignored the clear trail and pointed to the west. 'That's the way he'll go sooner or later, probably to Bitter Ridge. If we're lucky, we may be able to get there before him and lay on a little welcoming party for him.'

They gigged their mounts, pushed them as hard as they dared over the dry, crumbly face of the desert. Over their heads, against the blue-white mirror of the heavens, the buzzards wheeled like tattered strips of black cloth against the impeccable cloudless sky.

The morning was half gone and the heat head slowly climbed to its piled-up immensity, as they rode steadily west. Nothing relieved it. Around them, for mile upon endless mile, stretched the glaring white expanse of sand and alkali, its terrible monotony unrelieved by any hills or ridge of any real size.

The previous day had been a punishment to them, but this was even worse, making every breath a labour, sending pain shooting redly through their lungs. For most of the way they rode with their kerchiefs over their mouths and nostrils; heads bowed low over the necks of their mounts in an attempt to relieve the harsh, eye-searing glare thrown up by the sun.

They spoke little as they rode. They had been through far too much together these two men, for conversation to

27

be necessary between them, and out here in this desolate wilderness, where nothing grew to relieve the flat, rolling monotony, even talking was an effort, to be indulged in only when absolutely necessary. Their horses too were beginning to feel the strain of that terrible journey over the searing alkali. Already Doc Foran's mount was limping slightly. By the time they reached the far side of the desert, they would be fortunate if the horses were able to walk at all.

High noon; and the mountains seemed nearer now. All morning they had appeared to recede as they travelled, as if they were never going to get any closer. But this had clearly been an illusion brought about by the shimmering glare of the desert and the bright, cloudless mirror of the sky at their backs. There was still no change in the nature of the terrain over which they rode. Here the sun had sucked all moisture from the ground long ages before, mercilessly dehydrating it, and there was no rain to replace it.

Then, suddenly, there was the sharp smell of more dust in the air, more intense than before. Even with the neck-piece over his nose, Clem noticed it at once. There had been a rider here not long before, his mount kicking up the dust where it still hung in the air. Lifting his head, he stared out through the heat haze, letting his gaze wander from one horizon to the other.

'You smell dust?' murmured Doc.

'There's plenty in the air but I can't pick up any sign of him yet?'

'I'm guessing that this is a big bunch.' Doc screwed up his eyes against the sunglare. 'Too much dust for one man.'

He pointed off to one side. Clem followed the direction of his pointing finger and nodded tightly. There was a faint haze in that direction, barely discernible, except that it tended to obscure details on the far horizon. Different from the normal heat haze, this was a cloud of thrown-up dust which had been kicked high by the passage of horses across the desert.

'There!' muttered Clem a moment later. He gave a quick jerk of his head towards their right. His eyes three-quarter lidded against the glare, he managed to pick out the dark shapes of the riders, tightly bunched together, spurring their mounts fiercely across the alkali. They were more than five miles away, he judged, going out across the desert and from their distance and the direction in which they were travelling, he guessed that they had crossed the trail he and Doc were following, earlier that morning. The tightly packed bunch were curving away to the north-west behind the pattern of dust which partially hid them from view.

Doc sucked in his thin lips, nodded: 'That's them, all right,' he grunted, swinging back in the saddle. He drew the back of his hand over dry, parched lips and speculated long on the fast disappearing riders.

'Looks as though it could be a posse to me,' he observed finally. His eyes were half closed, shielding them from the sun. He dug his right hand into the pocket of his shirt, pulled out his tobacco pouch and he sat relaxed in the saddle as he built himself a smoke, glad of the chance just to sit, even though the hot sun laid a burning finger on their backs and shoulders.

If it is a posse, I wonder what they're doing this far from their home territory. The desert ain't the place to ride on a day like this.'

'Could be they're trying to find those Texas Dusters we were warned about,' murmured the other. He had the cigarette between his lips, spoke around it as he lit a match and applied the flame to the end. He sucked deeply on the smoke, grimaced a little as it burned his already parched tongue and lips.

CHAPTER TWO

NIGHT OF THE RUSTLER

The peaks were before them now, lifting clear and high. Clem glanced up at them, knew that he ought to feel a lifting of his spirit at seeing them so close, but strangely he didn't. The long journey over the desert had taken a lot out of them both and they had drunk very little during the two-day ride, even though every nerve and fibre of their being had cried out for water to wash the bitter coating of alkali dust from their throats. In that terrible country, it was better to ride dry than to sweat all of the water out of one's body.

They had seen no further sign of the big group of riders after the others had vanished from sight below a long, low ridge to the north-west and during the long, heat-filled afternoon, although they had kept a close watch on the trail that wound its tortuous path across the flats, it was clear that Goudie, the man they were trailing, had not moved across to link up with the main trail after his surprise swing away from the south.

The lie of the land here was of two different types. To

the east, along the way they had just ridden, lay the desert, a fifty-mile stretch of white, sun-caked alkali. Westward, the ground changed abruptly, became a wide tableland of rolling grass, undulating ridges and hills on the tops of which squatted clumps of low pine.

Good cattle country, reflected Clem, letting his tired gaze wander over it. Further along, maybe thirty miles distant, the country seemed to change again, but gradually this time, became more rugged, tall pinnacles of rock and black lava outflow, where boulders and buttes tumbled over each other to join the tall range of mountains that spiked the red glow of sunset and cut off this part of the territory from that which lay beyond, further to the west.

The trail from the north which wound around the far ledge of the desert, ran snakewise between these two starkly different types of terrain. Here and there it skirted an abutment of rock that thrust itself out from the grassy hills, jutting into the desertlands. Further on it branched, one leg going due south, levelling out over the small plain that bordered the hills, the other heading due west in the direction where they guessed Bitter Ridge to lie.

As they crossed the trail, the shadows grown long behind them, with a welcome coolness blowing out of the hills in to their faces, Clem searched the stage road for signs of fresh hoof-prints. There were some, but they lay between the deep wheel marks and had obviously been made by the stage horses and not by riders travelling alone.

'Judgin' by this stretch of cattle country,' said Doc, glancing out over the low hills, lifting his body slightly in the saddle, hands loose on the reins, 'I'd say there was another ten or fifteen miles at least to go before we hit town. No point in pushing the horses any further tonight, after what they've been through in the past two days. Reckon we ought to make camp hereabouts.'

Clem nodded in agreement. It was not likely that Goudie, if he was headed in this direction, hoping to reach Bitter Ridge, was in front of them after making that detour. More likely he was still back there to the south, hoping that he had thrown them off his trail by doubling back from the false trail he had so deliberately and obviously made for them.

'If Goudie is out there,' said Doc, walking his horse forward into the soft grass, 'he won't get far, even if he does reach this side of the desert during the night. His mount will be even more lame than ours after he's ridden all those miles over alkali.'

Darkness settled as they moved into the low hills, but for a long time after the sun had gone down and the flame-coloured glow in the sky had vanished, there was a pale, dim twilight that gave them enough light to see their surroundings by and they made good time, moving away from the trail. Looking back over his shoulder, Clem could make out the grey-white scar of the stage road along the very lip of the desert. It was empty as far as the eye could see in either direction and beyond it, out on the alkali flats that seemed to glow with a strange light, not a single thing moved.

He stretched himself tall in the saddle, felt the coolness of the breeze flow over him, loosening the tension that had built up in him over the long afternoon and evening. They passed a row of juniper bushes, then came to a narrow stream that cut down slantwise out of the hills, bubbling and boiling over a rocky bottom. From a nearby pine thicket, a whippoorwill whistled a shrill, high-pitched note over and over again, then detected their presence in the vicinity, and stopped.

Doc reined his bay and sat stiff in the saddle for a moment, listening. Then he turned. 'This looks like a good place to make camp. Plenty of shelter from that mesa. Shouldn't be too easy for anybody to spot a fire here and we're well off the trail.'

They tied the horses, built a fire from the brushwood and fried salt pork in a pan over it. Coffee was brewed, washing the dust and taste from their mouths and throats. Hunkering down, Clem speared a slice of pork with his bowie knife and thrust it into his mouth, chewing slowly on it.

Doc looked triumphantly at him. 'This is better than eating out there.' He pointed the blade of his knife in the direction of the alkali flats.

Clem nodded. Doc Foran, for all his reputation as a fast-shooting lawman, also prided himself on his cooking, a pride which Clem had found never to be misplaced. He speared another hunk of pork, ate it with relish, then drained the coffee in the iron cup.

As the light almost faded out, a chorus of coyote pups sprang up from the edge of the grasslands and in the far distance, the sound carried by the breeze that flowed down the dim sides of the hills, came the unmistakable lowing of a herd that had been bedded down for the night. The sound reminded Clem that they were entering cattle country. From there on to Bitter Ridge, they would be moving over the big spreads that reached out from the mountains in the west to the desert in the east.

Going down to the shallow stream, he washed the dust off his arms and face. The cold spring water stung his face where it had been freshly scorched by the terrible heat of the desert sun and he dried himself quickly. Doc looked up from the fire as he went back.

'I've just been trying to figure things out,' he said drily. 'Those riders we picked up back there about noon – suppose it wasn't a posse.'

Clem eyed him sharply 'What else do you reckon they could be? Not a trail crew. They'd never be that far in the desert.'

'Suppose it was those rustlers we heard so much about in Twin Buttes. They seemed to be heading over the desert towards the hills out there. And whoever they were, they seemed to be in a mighty big hurry.'

'Could still have been a posse from Bitter Ridge.'

Doc shook his head. 'If it had been, they'd have left their mark on the trail back yonder. But we saw no sign of a big party having come this way recently.'

'That's right, there was nothing.' Clem walked up to the top of the low mound nearby and stared off into the growing darkness. Around them everything was silent. The coyote pups had ceased their yammering and even the whippoorwill was quiet in the thicket.

'I know what you're thinking,' murmured Doc. 'Goudie may have joined them and it's just possible they may be back this way during the night.'

Clem nodded. 'There's a herd way out in that direction. This is just the kind of night for them to try something. From that gunsmith in Twin Buttes, I got the impression they're something to be feared in these parts. We may run into them during the night, they'd have to drive a herd pretty close to us if they mean to take them out into the desert.'

'I reckon we ought to take it in turns to sleep.' Doc got to his feet, joined the other on the ridge of ground. 'I don't fancy being ridden down by a stampeding herd of cattle.'

'Mebbe you're right.' Clem eased the twin Colts in their holsters. There was something about the night that filled him with a sense of unease. He could see nothing to explain it, nor could he hear anything, nothing to account for the nervous jumping of the nerves in his stomach where they had contracted into a hard, tight knot. 'I'll take the first watch,' he said.

Doc Foran hesitated, then gave a sharp nod, knowing

34

better than to argue. He went back to the fire, piled more brushwood on to it so that the flames leapt high into the air, giving little smoke, then laid out his bedroll and stretched himself out under the blanket, feet towards the fire. By force of habit, his gun lay on the ground near his right hand, ready to be snatched up at the first sign of trouble.

Clem walked over to a small upthrusting ledge of higher ground some yards from the fire where he would be outside the flickering orange glow of the flames, and settled down to watch. The stars were a brilliant powdering of light over his head, stretching from one horizon to the other in an unbroken arch. The thicket nearby, rustled drily in the soft breeze. A coyote howled dismally somewhere in the distant dimness, a wail that lifted to the heavens and sent a little shiver running along his spine. All around there was a dim, frosty glow over the country. By the fire, Doc was already asleep. The horses snickered softly to themselves in the shadows on the far side of the fire, near the stream.

Minutes drew long fingers of time away into the night. The coldness settled deeper into his bones, numbing his limbs, but he did not go down to the fire for warmth, not wanting to silhouette himself against the broad orange glow.

Once he got stiffly to his feet and made a wide walk around the camp, looking back over the country they had just covered. So far there was no sign of anyone moving up behind.

The movement brought some warmth and feeling back into his body. Going down to the bubbling stream, he knelt and drank his fill of the icy cold water, got to his feet and then paused as the faint, unmistakable hammer of gunfire drifted down to him from the north. The firing stayed brisk as he listened to it, not heavy smashing volleys, but carefully potted shots that barked through the night.

Going up on to the low rise, he tried to make out everything in that direction, straining his ears for the first sound that would tell him the herd they knew to be there was on the move, stampeded by those shots. The gunfire was undoubtedly a signal of things to come which the terrain about him, by the emptiness and the impression of tensely suppressed quiet, seemed to be heeding. He swung his gaze back to the trail. The bright starlight here laid a shimmering glow over the desert, picking it out from the darker foreground. He could just see the narrow-slashed greyness of the trail itself, the vaguest hint of greyness along the low hills and pine thickets. The wind flowed with its cool pressure against him and borne on it came the sound of more firing, rising swiftly to a savage crescendo.

As if warned by some hidden instinct, some part of him that never slept, Doc rolled out of his blankets near the fire at Clemn's back, caught up his gun, and walked forward until he stood beside him.

'What is it, Clem?'

'Gunfire. Sounds like trouble out there.'

'Rustlers?'

'Could be. That's the direction I figure the herd is. It's fairly steady fire too.'

The firing died away suddenly as if all opposition had been smashed. But the silence of the hills still had the beginnings of sound in it, a faintly growing rumble, like distant thunder on the horizon, but continuous and growing louder and more insistent. It was a sound known and feared by every rider and cowpuncher in the west. A herd on the move, countless tons of beef and muscle, 'smashing forward in a wide and irresistible wave. Nothing could stand in the way of a stampeding herd and remain alive. And this herd seemed to be heading right for the spot where they had made camp.

'They're headed for us.' Doc Foran snapped the words out through tightened lips, swinging round in the same instant. Clem followed him back to the camp. It was the work of minutes to stamp out the fire, roll up their blankets and saddle up the horses. And all the time they worked, the rumble of the approaching herd grew in their ears. Mounting, they pushed off the small plateau into the deep-cut canyon which lay just beyond the mesa, the high rough walls crowding close as they rode so that they could not ride abreast but were forced to move in single file with Clem in the lead, their legs scraping the rocky walls in places where the trail narrowed.

Halfway along the narrow canyon, with perhaps a quarter of a mile to go before they made the shelter of the timber, they heard more firing; this time it was short, sharp bursts of sound that echoed above the running thunder of the herd. Clem brought down his spurs against the horse's flanks and the animal broke into a dispirited run, shoes striking hard against the rock as it fought to keep its footing. The steep walls of the canyon began to drop down on either side, became more ragged. A moment later he rode out into the open and looked swiftly about him, eyes narrowed against the darkness.

Almost directly ahead of him he could make out the hazy cloud of dust thrown up by the herd as it rushed blindly onward, driven by the sharp and insistent hammering of the guns. A ragged burst of shots broke out and then ceased. The herd came at them down the side of one of the hills, visible now, a black mass of shadows that flowed like mud over the wide crest, curving and sweeping forward in a dark wave, blunted at the tip, with bulging sides that spread over the lee of the hill.

Clem looked anxiously at the timber just along the trail, knew that he and Doc had to reach it before the herd swung across and reached them or they would be finished, trampled to a smashed red pulp by those pounding hoofs.

Doc had also seen the danger, knew that the run of a stampeding herd was utterly unpredictable, that they could suddenly switch direction, depending on the whim of the natural leaders. Clem pointed, raked spurs along his mount's flanks, feeling sorry for the animal as he did so.

Crouched low over the creature's neck, he urged it forward, feeling fear ride with him, one mad leap along the trail and then another. He did not make any attempt to guide the horse. The reins hung free. His knees were pressed tightly together to maintain his grip on the horse. Ahead of them came the tidal wave of horns and pounding hoofs. He lifted his head to glance quickly in the direction of the oncoming herd, tried to judge whether or not they were going to make it. There was no doubt that the horses, tired as they were after that long haul over the desert, still possessed a turn of speed which gave them some advantage over those steers. This was familiar to men like Clem and Doc Foran; familiar and yet still terrifying in its utter savagery.

It was a desperate race for cover and safety. The horses responded magnificently, covering the ground swiftly. One false move on the smooth, slippery rocks that lay at the end of the canyon and it would have been the end for horse and rider. But the animals were both sure-footed beasts and less than half a minute later with the herd less than a quarter of a mile distant, they were in thick brush and Clem was ducking his head instinctively as a branch swung at him from the darkness.

Doc came crashing in at his back. They held their mounts steady in the cool darkness under the trees and the black mass of the herd swung past them less than ten feet away. Clem caught a glimpse of tossing heads, of needle-sharp horns that raked the heavens as the great heads heaved. Angry bellows came from the herd as it moved by in a seemingly endless stream, thrusting and pawing, the ground shaking as they moved on, running abreast of the two riders among the trees.

On the far side, through the dust cloud, Clem caught a faint glimpse of the men riding the herd. They were too far away for him to see any of their faces. He counted seven in all, men with their neckpieces pulled up over the lower halves of their faces; not so much to prevent them from being recognized, as to keep the dust of the drag out of their nostrils, dust churned up by more than four thousand pounding hoofs.

Gradually, the running steers thinned. Behind them, urging them forward, came three men, riding close on the stragglers, driving them forward with a series of high-pitched yells, discharging their guns into the air as they rode high in the saddle.

For a second, Clem's hands rested on the butts of the guns at his waist, fingers curled around the triggers. Then he forced himself to relax, holding his hands limply by his sides. There was no point in killing one or all of those three men, even though it would be one of the simplest things to do. They could shoot down all three and the sound of the shots would be barely discernible above the roar of the herd. The men were riding by without even suspecting their presence in the undergrowth among the trees on the edge of the canyon. When the last of the steers had gone, bawling, past, the thunder of the retreating herd dying away in the distance, Doc eased his mount forward, on to the trail, sat looking after the rustlers, a tight expression on his grizzled features.

'That's the first time in my life I've actually stood by and watched somebody breaking the law,' he said sharply, a harsh edge to his tone. 'We should have shot down some of those goddarned rustlers.'

Clem's answer came swiftly. 'I understand how you feel, Doc. But it wouldn't have helped. No sense in getting ourselves shot up by-that bunch until we know something more about 'em.'

'And where do you reckon we can find out?'

'In Bitter Ridge, maybe. In the meantime, we're after Goudie. Nobody else so far, although that may come in time. But there's no sense in getting ourselves mixed up in a range war that's really none of our business.'

'I'd sure like to make it my business,' grated his partner. 'A man can't stay in the middle when it comes to rustling. Next to cold-blooded murder, this is the worst crime in the territory according to my book. There they were, three of them, less than ten feet away, bringing up the rear. Three bullets would have finished them and their friends with the rest of the herd would've known nothing whatever about it until it was too late.'

'Could be. But it was best to take no chances. We'll learn as much as we can in town, at the same time keeping our eyes and ears open for Goudie. He may ride in some time tomorrow if he hasn't already linked up with those moonlighters.'

At daylight they saddled and returned to the trail, travelling back along it. Everywhere they saw signs of the stampede. Bushes had been flattened by the onslaught of that mighty rush of bone and muscle. Looking about him, Clem felt sobered by what he saw.

They crossed a shallow, gravel ford an hour after daybreak, still following the road. Now that they were closer to their destination, they travelled slow, letting the horses blow. Back in the desert, even back in Twin Buttes, they had felt urgency inside them, had felt the need for haste. But now, with the desert at their backs they had both acquired a deep patience, so that time did not seem

40

to matter much.

The first sun was high above the stiff pine tops when they came upon the scene of the gunfight of the previous night. Clem reined his mount at the top of the high slope and stared down into the lush green valley which lay spread out in front of him. This was evidently where the herd had been bedded down when the rustlers had struck suddenly and in force.

Switching his gaze to the right, he noticed the three horses standing close together near a solitary outcrop of rock. They still had saddles on them but were riderless and there was no sign of their owners.

He pointed them out to Doc Foran. 'Reckon we'd better get down there and take a look around.'

They put their mounts to the steep slope, the horses picking their way sure-footed over the treacherous ground. At the bottom they came on two of the riders, men who had been guarding the herd, lying face-downward in the lush grass. Dismounting, Clem went over to them, turned each man over gently, noticed the deep red stain on their shirts where they had been shot in the back, and felt the cold stiffness in their bodies. He stood up and shook his head in answer to Doc's inquiring glance.

'Both dead,' he said harshly. 'They never had a chance. Shot in the back and neither has his guns drawn. They must have been shot down from somewhere in the hills, without warning.'

Doc nodded, turned his head slowly. 'There should be a third man somewhere around.'

It was Doc who came across the third man. There was a trail of blood that led across the grass to a small creek which ran across the meadow and it was here that they found the third rider. He had been shot in the shoulder and had managed to drag himself to the creek, where he had tried to wash the wound and had then lost consciousness. Doc went down on one knee beside him, lifting his head and shoulders gently.

'How bad is he hit?' asked Clem.

'Pretty bad. He's lucky to be still alive. Must have lost a lot of blood, lying here all night.'

'Reckon you can fix it?'

'He's still got the slug in his shoulder. It'll have to come out as soon as possible. No time like the present, I guess, while he's still unconscious. The pain is going to be pretty bad.'

'Need any help?' Clem stood hesitantly by.

'You'll find a bottle of whiskey in my saddlebag. Bring it over here, will you.'

Wonderingly, Clem brought the whiskey and gave it to Doc, who must have seen the look on his face, for he said: 'This ain't for me, young fella. But I got to have something antiseptic if I'm to start probing inside his shoulder for that bullet. Otherwise, he'll die for sure.'

He poured the raw spirit liberally over the wound and then over the blade of his bowie knife. Then he went down on one knee beside the man, pulling the shirt away from the whole of his body. Not an easy job. The bullet could be lodged anywhere near the bone and if the man recovered consciousness, there would be nothing they could do for him but give him some of the raw liquor and hold him down while the job was finished.

'It looks a pretty raw wound,' said Clem, watching closely.

Doc nodded. 'That's a good sign in a case like this. It means the slug has gone in at an angle. Probability is that it hit the bone and slipped off it, going deeper into the flesh. If it had gone right in, with just a small hole showing, it would have embedded itself in the bone for sure and we'd have the devil's own job getting it out.'

Clem watched as the other probed in the deep wound

with the tip of the knife. There were several men who rode the wide trails who could carry out doctoring feats such as this and Doc Foran was one of the best. Whether or not he had been a genuine doctor before Clem had met up with him, he did not know. But there was a certain professional touch about the way he worked which suggested that he was used to working with better instruments than this.

The minutes drifted by; long, silent things. Once, the man stirred and the cracked lips opened as a deep moan escaped from them. Clem reached forward with his hands to get a hold on the other's shoulders if he did come out of the deep pit of unconsciousness into which he had sunk, but the other's head dropped to one side again and Doc Foran gave a nod of satisfaction.

He worked on slowly now, gently moving the tip of the blade more deeply into the wound. His face was set in concentration, the lines around his mouth and eyes etched a little more deeply into the leathery skin. But there was a rock steadiness to his hands as they moved carefully.

'If we can get the slug out and he does come round, we might be able to get some information out of him.' The other looked up for a moment at Clem. 'He was shot from the front, so there's a distinct possibility that he may have seen some of his attackers. He may even be able to identify some of them for us.'

'Even though it's really none of our business,' muttered Clem.

'Well, we could tell the sheriff in Bitter Ridge when we get there. They might even be able to follow the tracks of that herd if they moved out across the desert close to the spot where we camped.'

A moment later Doc Foran sucked in his cheeks. 'Here it is.' He gave a slight twist to the blade and a moment later brought up something into the palm of his hand, holding it out to Clem.

'Forty-five slug,' said Clem laconically. Just what I would have expected.'

He tore several strips from the man's shirt, poured a little more whiskey into the wound, then packed it with the strips of cloth, binding it tightly. 'That ought to hold until he can be taken into town.' He straightened up, then looked out over Clem's shoulder. 'Looks like we've got company.'

Clem turned. A group of riders were bearing down on them from the north, skirting the edge of the smooth rise. One of the leading riders pointed in their direction and the others spurred their mounts forward. The men checked their mounts ten yards away and the man who led them, a tall Texan with flowing white hair sat easily in the saddle, looking down at them with a casualness that was more than casual.

'That's Dunner,' said one of the men who sat at the old man's shoulder. 'That's his mount back there with the other two.'

'You seen anything of two men back there?' The Texan nodded towards the hills.

Clem got to his feet, nodded. 'They're both there – and they're both dead,' he said harshly. 'We found them as we rode down off the rise.'

The other eyed them curiously now. 'Where are you from?' he asked softly, but for all the quietness of his voice, there was a veiled note of menace in it which could be readily detected.

'Back east,' said Doc, equally softly. 'We rode out from Twin Buttes two days ago. Heading towards Bitter Ridge.'

'And did you see anything of the men who rustled my cattle through the night and shot down my men?' A hardness came into the old man's tone.

'Sure they did,' broke in the man beside him. He spoke

harshly, locking his gaze with Clem's. 'They're two of the men who did it. Why not ask 'em where they drove the herd? This is the first time that we've come across two of them and—'

'Quiet, Moray,' said the other, without turning his head. 'I'll ask the questions. If they're two of the rustlers we know what to do with 'em and they won't be running away. But it ain't likely that they would stay around after the others had gone, waiting to be picked up.' He dismounted as he spoke and walked across to them, glanced down at the wounded man lying near the creek in the long grass. He noticed the fresh bandages around the injured man's shoulder, looked up at Doc Foran and nodded in under-standing. 'You bandaged him up?'

'That's right,' Doc nodded. 'He was bleeding badly when we found him, must've crawled here after he'd been shot, maybe tried to bathe his wounds. I've done all that I can for him, I've got the slug out.' He held the piece of lead out to the other. 'Colt forty-five,' he said loosely. 'You won't get anything from that.'

'No, I guess not. You seem to have made quite a profes-sional job of that. You a doctor?'

'Not any longer. But I still know how to treat bullet wounds or mend broken limbs. A man doesn't ride the trails for thirty years without learning to do that.'

The other seemed satisfied with the answer, for he nodded slowly and grinned. 'The name's Cawdrey. I own this spread.' He turned to his companions. 'These men are all right.'

'We saw your herd being rustled during the night,' Clem said quietly. He nodded towards the south-east. 'They drove them along the trail over the hills, then they must have cut across the desert. We'd made camp a couple of miles from here and it was around midnight when we heard the shooting and then the stampede. We had to get under cover or we would have been trampled down.'

'I suppose it's too much to hope that you recognized any of the men with the herd?'

Clem shook his head. 'We're strangers here. We wouldn't know any of them even if we had seen their faces. But they all wore their neckpieces over their mouths and it was pitch dark at midnight with no moon.'

Cawdrey nodded tightly. His silver hair shone in the sunlight where it flowed from beneath the wide-brimmed hat he wore. 'This isn't the first time we've been hit by those rustlers. And many of the other spreads have been hit, too, during the past three years. We try to catch them but they leave no tell-tale tracks, even in the desert. We've managed to follow the trail for a little way, then we lose it.'

'Why don't you get a posse together and ride out after them?' asked Doc.

'That's a lot easier said than done, I'm afraid. We've tried in the past to hunt them down, but the desert is a mighty big place and there's plenty of evidence that they only use that route as a feint, that they turn and move off into the hills to the north. They're honeycombed with so many old mine workings that we'd never stand a chance of locating them and even if we did, they could hold off an army of lawmen in there without much trouble.'

'So the only chance you've got is to lay a trap for 'em, catch them just as they attack a herd.'

'That idea, I like,' mused the other. 'But they seem to know when we've got a watch out for them. They don't attack any herd when we have a score of men watching from the hills close by, ready to take them when they come. They move further afield then and attack another ranch, a long distance away, maybe even a ranch from which we've drawn men to guard one particular herd. When they know your plans like that, there's nothing you can do.'

'And how do they know this?' asked Clem, interested.

The old Texan shrugged. 'Who knows? They maybe have spies in town, picking up every scrap of information. Could be they even have a man among our force.'

'You've considered that?'

'Sure, but you can't check on every man you hire.' He glanced appraisingly from Clem to Doc Foran and then back again. 'How would you like to sign on my payroll? Since last night's work, I've lost two good men and probably a third.' He looked down at the wounded man at his feet. 'I need two men at least to replace them. Forty dollars a month and keep.'

'Riding herd or fighting?' asked Doc, his tone to the point.

'Less of the first and more of the last.'

'We'll think it over,' said Clem, before Doc could speak. 'But in the meantime, we have business in Bitter Ridge. Which way is it?'

The other paused, eyed him shrewdly, then lifted a hand and pointed almost due west, across the plain. 'That way,' he said, 'about ten miles. Just over the rise, you'll hit a trail that will take you right into town.' He paused, then went on: 'I feel that I owe you both a favour. If there's ever anything I can do, let me know.'

'Thanks.' Clem walked back to his horse, climbed slowly into the saddle. 'We'll remember that. In a country like this, it's good to have a friend one can count on.'

'They know me in town,' said the other. He spoke authoritatively, but there was nothing boastful in his tone. He was simply stating a fact. Just mention my name if you're in trouble.'

'You figure we might run into trouble in Bitter Ridge?' asked Clem, remembering the tension they had found in Twin Buttes.

'Could be. Who knows? These frontier towns are still

lawless, even though they have a sheriff and they're supposed to be law-abiding. We tend to steer clear of them, unless we're forced to go in.'

'Thanks for the warning. The same sort of thing happened at Twin Buttes.'

'There's a bad town,' agreed Cawdrey, nodding. He seemed to be speaking with the gravest kind of care, as if weighing each of his words before uttering them. 'Even the hills here house bandits and outlaws. It would take an army to flush them out. Now, about a job—'

'We'll think about it,' said Clem again. He wheeled his mount, pulling its head around sharply, kicking heels to its flanks. They rode over the rise, paused at the top to look back. Two men had dismounted and were lifting the injured man across one of the saddles. Two others had picked up the dead men and were tying them across the pommels of their mounts. Only Cawdrey was turned in their direction and following their departure.

'What do you think of these rustlers?' asked Doc, as they put their mounts down the far slope, joining the trail two minutes later. 'You reckon they could be men from one of the other outfits?'

'Could be. After all, they'll have to get rid of those steers once they've driven them into the hills, even if they manage to change the brands. It would be a long drive east to the railhead.'

'And if Goudie has friends in this territory, then he'll have joined up with them by now.'

'Perhaps. Once we hit Bitter Ridge we'll stick around for a while and wait for him to ride in for a bust. He's sure to do that sooner or later, and when he does, we'll be ready for him.'

The trail led them over rich grasslands, past the edges of two spreads, the wire glittering in the sunlight, where it was strung from one pole to another. Once they saw a large herd in the distance, beyond one of the wires. Then they were riding along the bank of a sluggishly-flowing river, with a deep sandy bottom, a river that led them west to Bitter Ridge.

The town stood in a fold between two hills, the wide stage line running through it along the main street, then out the other side and into the hills, winding between high ridges before it vanished along the tall stretches of higher ground.

Riding along the main street of the town, the two men made a picture for many eyes to follow. Clem felt curious stares on him, but gave no indication that he was aware of them. The street seemed oddly empty as they drifted along it, eyes alert. A few horses were tethered to the rails outside the stores or the saloons, and there were several men sitting on the boardwalks, their faces hidden in the shadows.

'Looks almost as if they're expecting trouble,' whispered Doc without turning his head.

'Another town like Twin Buttes.' Clem let his gaze move from one side of the street to the other. Halfway along the main street he picked out the hotel. It was a tall, two-storeyed building of red brick, most of the windows over-looking the street. There was a covered-in walk around the lower floor and a veranda that ran around the upper floor.

At the side of the hotel, under a low archway, were the livery stables and they rode in, ducking their heads as they passed beneath the arch. Handing their horses over to the man who drifted out of the shadows, they went into the hotel and up to the desk. The clerk, a thin-faced man, eyed them curiously.

'Got a couple of vacant rooms?' asked Clem.

The other paused, then nodded. 'I guess so.' He turned the register for them to sign their names, glanced down at what they had written, then took down two keys from the board behind him and slid them over the top of the walnut desk.

'Upstairs and at the far end of the passage,' he said, pointing. 'You put your mounts into the stables?'

'They've been taken care of,' muttered Doc. He turned on his heel and followed Clem up the stairs and along the passage.

Clem's room was large and, as he had thought, opened out on to the wide balcony. He went to the windows and pushed them open in an attempt to relieve the heat in the room. There was a low iron bed in one corner and the large wash-basin near the window with a jug of water standing in it.

'Guess I'll wash up before supper,' said Doc. He left the room and moved along the passage to his own. Clem heard the door of the other's room close a moment later, then went over to the bed and stretched himself out on it, trying to rest his mind as well as his body, but that was not too easy in this strangely complex situation in which they had suddenly found themselves. They had ridden out here following the trail of one man, Sam Goudie, robber and killer, a man with a price on his head. They had followed him into Twin Buttes and then lost him because of that storm which had blown up without warning and hammered against them along the trail, making them lose precious minutes.

Now, after trailing him across the alkali flats, they had arrived in this area, only to find that, unless they were extremely careful, they would find themselves caught up in something far bigger than merely hunting down one man with a record of murder and stage robbery.

It would certainly simplify matters if Goudie should come riding alone into town that day or the next. Then they would be able to take him, ride back east with him and see that he was tried for his crimes and convicted.

Then their part in the case would be over, everything would be closed. Maybe when that happened, they might be able to come back there and help in cleaning the territory of these Texas Dusters, who seemed to be riding off with most of the big herds, with everyone in the vicinity seemingly powerless to stop them.

On that long journey across the burning white alkali, he had looked forward to meeting this man in Bitter Ridge, of coming face-to-face with him and challenging him to draw.

There was the sound of Doc splashing in the water, coming from the next room and outside, in the street, the usual sounds of a town such as this. Wagons began to creak as a small train moved into town. Vaguely, he found himself wondering if it was the same one they had noticed in Twin Buttes getting ready to move west. This was a vast and expanding country now, with hordes of small wagons heading to the rich country of California that lay far to the west on the coast of the Pacific. At times in the past he had felt those self-same urges in him, the desire to ride west and keep on riding, following new trails, until he came to that rich, golden country. If it was as good there as they said it was, he could understand these thousands of men and women enduring all of the tremendous hardships of the trail, to get there.

Already, the Red Man had been pushed back from the wide prairies which had once been his hunting grounds and the tremendous herds of buffalo which had roamed this country were fast disappearing. But change had to come if the country was to fulfil its destiny. There had to be this outward urge in the people if civilization was to reach out from its hold in the east and envelope the whole of America.

He felt a slight bitterness in him as he remembered the reason for him being there. So long as there were men like

Goudie and these Texas Dusters around, then progress was bound to be halted. Crooked sheriffs and lawmen, men whose job it was to uphold the law, really working hand-in-hand with the gamblers and big cattle men, taking over whole towns, making it impossible for decent men and women to live in peace.

It would make things simpler for Doc and himself if Goudie had merely ridden into Bitter Ridge as a place to hide, hoping to keep one jump ahead of them. If he had joined up with this notorious gang of outlaws, then it was not going to be easy to lay their hands on him. He did not fancy having to go up against this gang without plenty of outside help. Even though the law in this town and certainly most of the larger ranches in the surrounding territory might pitch in and help, particularly Cawdrey, so far these people did not seem to have had any success in tracking down these rustlers and there was no guarantee that he could help any further.

Outside, there was the sound of a group of riders coming into town. They stopped almost immediately opposite the hotel room and as he lay there he tried to remember what lay there. Not one of the saloons, he felt sure of that. The sheriff's office. Probably a posse riding back after an unsuccessful hunt for the Texas Dusters. He half rolled in the bed to rise and go over to the window. Then he heard the clatter of boots in the hall down below and a few moments later, after a dull murmur of conversation, the steps came up the stairs and along the passage outside his room, pausing in front of the door. He heard the clerk's voice: 'This is where they are, Sheriff. Are you sure there're two of 'em?'

A gruff voice said harshly: 'Pretty sure, Mr Valance. Now you'd better go back to your desk, just in case there's trouble. These men are pretty desperate. Don't know why they ride into town in this bare-faced way.' There was theunmistakable sound of footsteps hurrying away along the thinly-carpeted hall and then a thunderous knocking on Clem's door, knuckles rapping solidly. The harsh voice called:

'All right, you in there. Open up in the name of the law.'

CHAPTER THREE

FALSE TRAIL

The knocking on his door came again, more thunderously this time and the voice repeated the command. Clem rose, went over to the door and turned the key in the lock, opening it. Three men stood outside, one with the badge of a sheriff pinned on his shirt. He held a gun in his hand, pointing it at Clem.

'That's better.' Reaching forward with one hand, he unbuckled Clem's gunbelt so that it fell to the floor of the passage. Out of the corner of his eye, Clem saw that two other deputies were pushing their way inside Doc's room. He heard Doc give an angry bellow, and then a moment later he was herded into the passage, still dabbing at his face with the rough towel, naked from the waist up.

'What is this?' snapped Clem harshly. He locked his gaze with that of the sheriff.

'You'll find that out soon enough.' There was a sarcastic note in the sheriffs voice. He turned to his men. 'All right, boys. Take them over to the jail and put 'em in the cells. I'll take a look over these rooms, just in case they were stupid enough to leave any evidence lying around.'

'Now hold on there,' called Doc. 'What charge are you

taking us in on? You can't just arrest a man like that without giving any reason.'

'Can't I? Well, when it comes to men like you, I'm doing
just that.' One of the men standing just inside the doorway
grinned. 'What did you expect, Sheriff, that they'd admit
they were riding with the Texas Dusters?'

'The Texas Dusters.' For a moment the surprise was so
strong in Clem's mind that anyone might have been
forgiven for thinking from the look on his face that he was
guilty of the charge they had laid against him.

'That's right.' The sarcasm increased and the sheriff
gave a quick nod. 'Or are you aimin' to tell us that you
ain't heard of 'em?'

'Sure we've heard of them. We heard about them back
in Twin Buttes and we saw them herding off part of the
Cawdrey bunch.'

The sheriff's eyes slitted at that and there was a speculative gleam in them. He gave a curt nod to the men in the
doorway and two of them came forward and grabbed Clem
by the arms, forcing them to his sides. It was useless to argue.
Clem realized that instantly. No chance to make a fight for
it, not with those drawn guns levelled on them. There was no
doubt, judging by the look on the sheriffs features that he
was just itching for a chance to pull the trigger.

Shrugging, Clem stepped out into the passage. Doc was
thrust forward beside him. Turning to face the sheriff,
Clem said quietly: 'You're making a big mistake about this,
Sheriff.'

'We'll see,' muttered the other curtly. He went inside
the room and Clem and Doc were taken down the stairs,
through the lobby of the hotel, with the clerk watching
wide-eyed from behind the desk. Out in the street, a small
knot of people had gathered to watch, attracted by the
horses in front of the hotel. Clem saw them move forward
as he and Doc were led into the street, saw the anger on

their faces and thought: Good God, even they believe that we're two of those rustlers.

Clem felt the stirring of tension in his body, watching the threatening movement of the small crowd as they moved around in a semi-circle as if to cut them off from the sheriff's office on the other side of the street.

'What you figuring on doing with them two varmints?' called a voice from the crowd.

'We saw what those Texas Dusters did to Clements,' shouted another man thickly. He pushed his way forward to the front of the crowd. A tall, black-bearded man, eyes slitted with a feral hate. 'Reckon we know how to handle them, deputies, and we can save you a lot of trouble, too.'

'String 'em up.' The cry went up and was echoed by a scattering of voices along the street, sweeping through the watching crowd like a prairie fire. Clem narrowed his eyes, flicked a sharp glance towards the deputies, then back to the crowd. There were troublemakers among them, he reflected, trying to stir up the others. Why, he wasn't sure. Certainly they couldn't be men in league with the rustlers. Maybe misguided men who had lost cattle or relatives because of the activities of the Texas Dusters. But most of the crowd seemed uncertain of what to do, particularly as the deputies had now drawn their guns and were standing close beside Doc and himself.

'Just a minute,' shouted one of the deputies harshly. He moved forward and the crowd fell back in front of him. If these two men are part of that outfit, then we'll soon find out and then the law will take its course. These men aren't going to wriggle out of this. The sheriff is up there in their rooms. He'll find something to convict 'em, if it's there. Then there'll be time enough for a necktie party.'

In spite of this, there were still sullen murmurings from the crowd and Clem could sense their mood. It meant trouble for Doc and himself, even if they did succeed in getting them over to the jail safely. It wouldn't take much to stir these folk up into a truly ugly mood and there could well be a lynching mob on its way to bust them out of the jail and string them up from the nearest tree.

The black-bearded man stepped forward, his boots shuffling in the dust of the street. He glared up at Clem. 'Can't say I've seen either of these two men around these parts before. But they rode in a little while ago, headed off the Cawdrey ranch, saw 'em myself about a mile from town. Did hear, too, that Cawdrey lost a lot of beef during the night, driven off the hills and out into the desert.'

'Then it must've been the same bunch,' agreed someone else among the watching men.

Clem cleared his throat. 'That's no proof that we were with them,' he called loudly. 'Would we be foolish enough to ride openly into town if we belonged to that rustling outfit?'

'You might,' sneered the big man in front of him, thrusting his head forward until his face was only an inch from Clem. If you figured that you might be able to pick up some information in town. We know that the Texas Dusters have been getting advance information about any plans we make to capture 'em. Ain't that true, Jake?'

'It sure is,' nodded one of the deputies. He flung Clem a sharp look. 'Could be you're right. But Sheriff Howell will find that out and then we'll know what to do with these two – and we'll do it legal.'

'You mean that even if they are guilty, you're going to wait until the circuit judge gets here, and then they'll maybe be taken to Storman City.'

'You'd better have a talk with Howell about that. We're just obeying orders. Now step on one side, Ben, unless you want us to arrest you for obstructing the law.'

'Cut the palaver,' said the other nastily. 'We want action, not a lot more words from you. Now that we've got two of 'em, make 'em talk, tell us where their hideout is. Just let

57

me have 'em for an hour and I'll soon find out where they've got all of that beef stacked away in the hills.' He moved forward threateningly, then stopped as the gun in the deputy's hand lowered, the barrel pointing at the other's chest.

Just hold it there, Ben. I don't want any trouble, but if you got any complaint about the way this is being done then you'll have to take it up with Howell.'

'Then by God, I'll do that,' snarled the other thickly. He hesitated for a moment, a gleam of decision in his narrowed, deep-set eyes. Then he stepped back into the crowd, muttering ominously, the deputy's gun still on him. For a moment there was an uneasy silence in the hot, dusty street. Then the deputy turned to the two prisoners.

'All right. If you want to keep your skins until you've had a trial, you'd better get over there to the jail. I ain't going to guarantee holding these folk back much longer.'

Shrugging, Clem walked between the men across the street, listening to the muted muttering of the crowd at his back. He glimpsed the look on Doc's face and knew what thoughts were running through the other's mind at that moment. Here they were, a couple of rangers, caught in this god-forsaken frontier town and suspected of being in league with the most notorious gang of rustlers in the whole of the west. If the situation wasn't so serious, it might have been funny.

He tightened his lips, followed the men into the sheriff's office, then through into the narrow passage that led to the back of the building. Here, the jail had been built, strong steel bars, set well in the foundations of the building. There were six cells, three on each side of the passage. All were empty.

Turning the key in one of the cumbersome cell locks, the deputy motioned them inside, slammed the door hollowly behind them and locked it once more. 'Reckon the sheriff will be across to have a talk with you two *hombres*,' muttered the other. He stood for a moment outside the cell, then turned on his heel and walked off. Clem heard the clatter of his booted heels on the floor of the passage, then the sound of the door at the far end, leading into the sheriffs office, closing with a hollow sound.

The cell was not large. There was a solitary window set in one wall, looking out on to a narrow alley at the side of the building. Peering along it, Clem managed to make out the roughened brick of the building opposite and there was a horse standing at the far end of the alley where it opened out on to the main street. But apart from this, there was no sign of life out there. The sunlight was almost gone now, but there was still a bright glow of twilight in the sky and a warmth that came off the walls where the sun had laid a hot finger on them during the long day.

He went back into the middle of the cell and sat down on the edge of the bunk that ran along one wall.

'No chance of getting out that way,' he said quietly. 'We seem to have landed ourselves in a pretty mess this time. If only Goudie knew of this, he'd be laughing his head off. Him still on the loose and the two lawmen tracking him down in jail on a charge of rustling.'

'I didn't like the look of that crowd out there,' said Doc pointedly. He fumbled in his pocket and managed to find his tobacco pouch, rolled himself a smoke, then handed the pouch to Clem. 'Maybe that sheriff is a straight man, and maybe those deputies he has will do as he says, but they might not stand a chance holding off that mob if they decide to get nasty. There were some troublemakers among 'em when they took us out into the street. Somebody wants us strung up, maybe somebody knows who we are.'

'You figure that Goudie might be in town already then?'

'Seems like it. He's probably got friends here, that

could be why he took that trail over the desert. It ain't likely he'd do that just to get to another town. He must have had a reason for wanting to get here. With us strung up as cattle thieves, he'd be safe. Nobody else would think of looking for him here.'

'Then we've got to convince the sheriff of the truth of our story.'

'That might be easier said than done,' said Doc tightly. 'So far, there's only our word that we're lawmen. And we know that the wanted posters on Goudie haven't got this far. We don't have much evidence against him.'

'What about Cawdrey? He could testify that we aren't part of that Texas Dusters bunch.'

'And you reckon that the sheriff is going to send out to him, just on the chance that he might clear us of this trumped-up charge? Those townsfolk would have been stirred up by the trouble-makers long before he managed to get there and back.'

The sound of the door at the end of the passage opening, jerked Clem's head around. A moment later there was the sound of footsteps coming closer and the sheriff appeared outside the cell.

'Well,' said Clem, getting to his feet and walking over to the door of the cell. 'Did you find anything in our rooms to link us with the Texas Dusters?'

'No.' The other shook his head. 'But I didn't really expect to. You wouldn't be as stupid as that if you meant to ride brazenly into town.'

'Listen, Sheriff,' said Doc Foran, coming forward. 'We can't prove that we are just law-abiding citizens, same as you can't rightly prove we've got anything to do with that gang of rustlers. But I reckon you know Cawdrey.'

'Tracy Cawdrey? The rancher?' There was a look of surprise on the other's face. 'Sure I know him. Reckon everyone in the territory knows him.'

'Then get to him. He can tell you that we aren't part of that crowd. We saw part of his herd being run off during the night when we were camping on his spread. We found two of his riders dead this morning and a third with a bullet in his shoulder. He can tell you what you want to know. He even offered us jobs on the ranch to replace those two men who had been killed. He wouldn't do that unless he was pretty sure of us.'

'If that's so, why didn't you take the jobs? Why ride on into Bitter Ridge?'

'We had some business to attend to in town,' said Clem quietly.

'What sort of business?'

'That's our affair,' muttered Doc. He turned away from the other, walked back to the bunk and sat down on it.

Sheriff Howell stiffened 'That sort of attitude ain't going to get you very far,' he said sharply. 'That crowd out there are shouting for your blood. Those rustlers have plenty of enemies in town and now that they've got it into their heads that you're in with them they'll—'

'There's something wrong here, Sheriff,' said Clem thoughtfully. 'Why should they think we know anything about the Texas Dusters? We've just ridden into town and put up at the hotel. Who swore out the papers for our arrest? Who's at the back of this attempt to get us lynched?'

'I'm sorry,' Howell said, 'but I can't tell you that. All I know is that you're both strangers here and that you rode in from the desert. There are also witnesses who claim that you met up with a bunch of men out there and you were seen near the place where Cawdrey's herd was attacked and run off into the hills.'

'That's a lie,' snapped Doc. 'We're—' He made to go on and then caught the look in Clem's eye and stopped abruptly.

Howell swung sharply on him. 'Go on,' he said harshly, 'what were you going to say there. What are you?'

'It was nothing,' muttered the other. He had taken Clem's warning. There was always the possibility that- the sheriff himself might be in with these rustlers and it would be foolish to give away the fact that they were rangers, looking for Goudie, until they were sure of things.

'Then I reckon you'd better think up some good reason for being here in Bitter Ridge,' said the sheriff ominously. 'You know what these lynch mobs can be like when they're really roused. Ain't much that can stop 'em.'

'And you'd just sit back and let 'em come and take us. Is that it?' said Doc, glaring at the other through the bars.

Howell shrugged. 'I'm here to keep the law in this town and I aim to do that to the best of my ability. But I can understand the feelings of those men and women out there. Barely a week goes by without somebody being shot down by these killers. Nearly every rancher in the territory has lost cattle. Slowly, this place is being ruined by these rustlers. You can't blame folk if they decide that the due processes of the law are taking too much time over things and that while we're talking and arguing among ourselves, other men are being shot in the back from ambush.'

'Then why not get in touch with Cawdrey? At least, he can tell you whether or not we're the cold-blooded killers you make us out to be; whether Doc here saved the lives of one of those men who were shot during the night.'

Sheriff Howell backed away, keeping one hand close to the gun at his waist. 'I'll do my best to get in touch with Cawdrey, but I can't promise anything. You saw what it's like in town since you got here. Those folk out there are likely to run wild at any time, especially if they get some whiskey into them and at the moment, that's what seems to be happening down at the saloons. I need all the men I can get to keep an eye on the town and on you in particular.'

'Can't you send one man? If he hurries, he'll be there and back before morning.'

'I ain't promising anything,' muttered the other. He turned and walked quickly back along the passage, like a man, thought Clem, who was hurrying from his troubles, trying desperately to put them behind him.

There were loud voices in the street an hour later, sounding from not far off. Through the window of the cell it was just possible to see the stars, glimmering brightly in the night sky. From the distance came the weird, undulant howling of a coyote. Nearer at hand, a couple of dogs barked fiercely at the sound.

From the direction of the saloon there came the sudden shouting of voices, some singing an old Southern song at the top of their voices, but others muttering in anger. Once Clem thought he heard a solitary voice that seemed to run like a shining thread though the general tapestry of sounds, exhorting the men to violence. It was a harsh, but eloquent voice, one that could sway crowds to its bidding and he guessed that it boded ill for Doc and himself.

The singing and yelling in the saloon continued without abatement. Clem listened to it apprehensively. It was not the usual saloon bar stuff, although to an ordinary listener it would appear that there was nothing but friendship and good feeling towards everybody. Only to an acute ear would the harshness in the singing, the fact that there was too much noise, become apparent; and the possible reason behind it be guessed. Whoever was whipping up the feeling in this crowd, wanted to fill the town with noise so that it would hide something.

'What do you think, Clem?' Doc got up and moved across to the window, trying to peer out into the dark alley, to make out any movement in the street in the far distance.

'It's bad. They're up to something and it won't be to our benefit. I'd sure like to know who's behind all of this.'

'Goudie. It makes sense that he's the one who wants us out of the way.'

'Sure, but I doubt whether Goudie would have had time yet to get so well in with these people that he could whip them up like that. Besides, I've been listenin' to that singing and talking down there at the saloon. I can just pick out occasionally, some voice trying to get them moving. It wasn't Goudie's voice, I'd stake my life on that.'

'But there isn't anybody else, Clem. We aren't known here and it's doubtful if there's anyone else we've run up against in the past here, somebody who had recognized us.'

Boots suddenly thumped the hollow boardwalk in the alley, coming closer. They paused a few yards from the window. Gingerly, Clem edged forward and glanced out. There was sufficient light for him to make out the man who stood in the middle of the alley, lighting up a smoke. When he lifted his head and peered into the darkness, Clem saw that he was a stranger. Not one of the men he had seen before in the crowd. After a few moments the drifter moved off along the alley and stood with his back against the wall at the far end, leaning nonchalantly against it, the smoke giving purpose to his apparent idleness.

For a long moment after that, nothing happened. Down the street the men in the saloon were singing. Around the jail, Bitter Ridge had quietened and there was only that uproarious sound to break the silence. Then there came the sound of a rider moving swiftly along the street, heading north. Cleni caught the rush of hoofs, then the fading of the sound into silence. That could have been the man Sheriff Howell had said he would send out to the Cawdrey place. Certainly the rider was heading in the right direction.

Looking along the alley, he noticed that the stranger was still there, his shoulders against the wall, the tip of his cigarette glowing redly in the darkness as he drew on it. Five minutes later there came the sound of footsteps coming his way along the boardwalk.

Clem stiffened as he saw the dark figure that stepped into the alley mouth and moved over to speak with the loafer. It was the tall, black-bearded man who had been the leading trouble-maker in the crowd when he and Doc had been arrested. There were two other men with him, moving into the shadows, eyeing the main street in both directions. The black-bearded man jerked a thumb in the direction of the jail, said something to the loafer that Clem was unable to hear, and the latter nodded his head emphatically, then moved off out of sight. Black-beard signalled to his two followers and they came slowly along the alley. There was a singleness of design, of purpose, about their approach that forced Clem back from the window, grabbing Doc by the arm and pulling him down on to the floor.

'Quickly!' he hissed. 'Down on your face and right against the wall.'

The other obeyed without question, throwing himself down, pressing his body close beside Clem's, hard against the stone wall of the cell. The sound of heavy footsteps came right up to the outside wall and they heard the harsh breathing of the man standing there. 'Right, boys,' muttered a tight voice that Clem recognized as belonging to the black-bearded giant. 'Get them and make no mistake. We may not be able to work up that crowd back there at the saloon into a killing fever.'

Something rattled against the bars across the window and out of the corner of his eye, Clem saw light glimmer bluely on the barrel of the revolver that was thrust through into the cell. It slanted downward and a moment later the deafening sound of shots boomed in the confined space of the cell. There was the acrid stench of burnt powder in Clem's nostrils and he heard a vicious whine as a ricochet spun off the floor and crashed through the door of the cell, striking the opposite wall of the passage.

More shots echoed through the windows of the other cells. Evidently the men were not sure which cell they were in and they were taking no chances, firing through the windows of them all. Savagely, Clem pushed himself against the wall immediately below the window, trying to press his legs tightly against his body. The gunman emptied his weapon, then stepped away from the window.

A pause, then the harsh voice said: 'Don't hear anything in there. Reckon we got 'em. If not, then we'll soon have the sheriff here and if they're still alive, we'll get the crowd here before first light.'

The footsteps receded into the distance along the alley and Clem let his breath go in quiet pinches, struggling to his feet. When he judged that it was safe to do so he peered cautiously through the window. He could see nobody out there in the alley and in the near distance, inside the saloon, the voices were still raised in their loud chorus and now he knew why the sound of the singing had stirred the uneasiness in his mind. It had been done so as to cover up the sound of the shots from the direction of the jail.

'You reckon they'll come back and try again?' Doc struggled to his feet and sucked a deep lungful of air down into his chest.

'They might. But it would be risky to try that again. They figure that if we ain't dead, then a lynch mob will soon rectify matters on that score.' He rubbed the stubble on his chin thoughtfully. 'I wonder who that black-bearded *hombre* is and why he's so almighty anxious for us to be killed. Seems he has a hand in this somewhere.'

'You reckon he might be one of the Texas Dusters, that

he's getting folk stirred up deliberately to have us strung up?'

'Sure looks that way right now.'

There was some shouting in the street now and a moment later he heard the loud knocking on the front door of the sheriffs office. There was no answer and whoever it was went away. Then, five minutes later the outer door was opened and there was the faint jangle of keys as someone came along the passage carrying a lantern. The man stepped outside the cell door and peered in. Slitting his eyes against the yellow glow of the lantern, Clem saw that it was one of the deputies who had brought them over to the jail.

'What's going on here?' demanded the other.

Swallowing his anger, Clem called out: 'Seems somebody out there is mighty anxious to finish us off without even waiting for that mob to come and get us. They tried to shoot us down through the windows.'

'You all right?'

'At the moment we are. But there's no telling when they'll come again and have another try for us, especially if they discover that we're still alive.'

'I'll warn the sheriff when he gets back?'

'Where is Sheriff Howell?'

'He rode out of town about an hour ago heading north. He didn't say where he was going, just that we had to keep an eye on you and make sure that no harm came to you until he got back.'

'That was thoughtful of him,' said Doc and there was a heavy irony in his tone. 'Seems he might be unlucky. Those men were talking of getting the mob over here before dawn. They sure mean business.'

'No cause to worry,' said the other, but he did not sound as confident as he tried to make out. 'There are six men coming over. They'll be in the office and if the mob do try to bust you out of jail for a lynching they'll have us to deal with.'

'And you figure that you can hold off perhaps a hundred men when they come?' Clem shook his head. 'You know, I don't think you believe we're part of this rustling gang at all. But that won't make it easy for you to stand up to that crowd when they come.'

'They're all wind and nothing else,' said the other uneasily. He glanced down at the rifle he carried in his other hand. 'They'll talk and maybe get drunk in the saloon, but that's as far as it will go.'

'I hope you're right,' Clem said. He paused, then, as the other made to move away, asked: 'That tall man with the black beard. Who's he?'

'You mean Ben Haswell. He owns one of the stores in town. Why do you ask about him?'

'Because he was one of the three men who came and tried to kill us just now. From what I could see from the window before they came, he had it all set up, with a man watching the main street from the end of the alley. He's also got those men in the saloon singing at the tops of their voices so it would drown out the sound of those shots.'

'Ben Haswell.' In the yellow glow from the lantern, the deputy shook his head slowly. 'You got it all wrong, mister. Sure, we know that Ben is mighty hot-headed at times, but he wouldn't do that.'

'Reckon you don't know him very well then,' grunted Clem laconically. He went back to the bunk and lowered himself on to it, staring straight ahead of him. After an uneasy moment, the deputy turned and went away, the flickering yellow light from the lantern fading along the passage. The end door closed and they were left with the silence again.

The rumble of voices in the saloon grew louder. There was the sudden tinkle of breaking glass, a bull-like roar and then a couple of gunshots that blasted in quick succession.

'Sounds as though the party is over and they're getting down to real business,' murmured Doc. He swung over to the window and looked out. 'Don't reckon they'll come this way if it's a necktie party. They'll come in the front entrance to make things look legal.'

There was a sudden ominous silence now outside. No laughter, no harsh yelling, no singing. It was as if a blanket had dropped around the cell, letting no sound through. Clem felt the muscles of his throat cord and contract. Tension gripped his body and his mind locked against thought. Then, in the distance, there was the sound of men walking along the main street, many men, coming in the direction of the jail.

'That mob's headed this way, deputy.' Clem shouted the words at the top of his voice. 'You going to leave us in here to get killed. At least you can give us our guns and the chance to defend ourselves.'

'Keep your mouth shut back there.' The deputy's voice reached them, muffled by the closed door at the end of the passage. 'We'll deal with 'em if they try anything here.'

'I reckon he won't have much choice in the matter,' murmured Doc softly. He looked across the cell at Clem. 'That crowd means business. They've been getting themselves all steamed up there in the saloon and now they're coming to make sure that we ain't around by the time the sheriff gets back.'

Clem nodded, went over to the door of the cell, gripping the iron bars with his hands, fingers curled about them tightly, knuckles standing out white under the skin with the pressure he was exerting. The ominous stillness began to press on them again. They could no longer hear even the shuffle of footsteps along the street.

'What do you reckon they's doing now?' asked Doc from further back in the cell. He moved to the window, peered out, then shook his head as he turned back. 'Nobody there.'

'They'll be waiting for somebody to step up and make the first move,' muttered Clem harshly. 'Nobody in that crowd wants to get himself shot by one of the deputies just for the honour of being first inside the building. I guess our hides aren't as important to them as that.'

The silence continued. Of a sudden, Clem had a clear, cold vision of that crowd of men standing in the street outside the sheriffs office, hard, bitter and angry men, some inflamed by drink, carefully nurtured by the trouble makers, ready for action. They would have been promised a lot to bust into the jail and get Doc and himself out, ride them out of town to the nearest tree where they would be strung up with a couple of lariats.

'You inside there, Cassidy?' The harsh voice broke the stillness, yelling from the front of the building.

A pause, then the deputy's voice answered. 'I'm here, Ben. Better get those folk out there off the street. Go back to your homes and leave the law to take care of this. You know that Sheriff Howell will be back before morning and then we'll try those two *hombres* in jail. I promise you they ain't going no place.'

'It ain't that we don't trust you, Cassidy.' The voice shouted the words, 'but we're all a little tired of words and no deeds. While we're standing here waitin' for somethin' to be done, those other raiders are probably stampeding more cattle into the hills. When is it going to stop?' There was a harsh murmur of sound from the crowd.

'Now I ain't going to warn you again, Ben. Or any of you out there. This is somethin' to do with the law and you ain't going to take it into your own hands to see that justice is done. If these men are guilty then—'

'We know they're as guilty as hell,' roared another voice. The owner sounded a little drunk. 'I say we bust down that door and drag them out. There's a fine tree just along the trail outside the town and I've got a brand new rope here.'

A drunken man, probably an honest, decent citizen most of the time, thought Clem bitterly. But something happened to men like that once they got a certain idea into their mind, an idea that was nurtured and played upon by evil men such as the black-bearded storekeeper, who seemed to be the leading trouble-maker out there. The old ways of violence that never seemed to change.

'You see how these folk feel, Cassidy. Now if you don't open that door peaceful like and let us in, we're going to come in by force and take those two men out. Better play it careful. We don't want to have to hurt you, and I don't see any sense in you getting hurt just to save their miserable skins.'

I'm not doing this to save them,' snapped Cassidy. 'I've got my orders from the sheriff. He'll say when they're to be taken out of here. Nobody else got that right.'

'No? Well we're taking it.' A momentary pause and then the man shouted: 'You heard what Cassidy said, boys. He ain't going to let us in peaceable, so we're going to have to bust our way in. Are you all with me? Do we take those two rustlers and string 'em up?'

There was a great shout from the crowd outside. Judging by the sound, he guessed that it had been one of the deputies who had fired the weapon.

'I ain't going to warn any of you again,' called Cassidy. 'That was the last warning you'll get. The next man who tries to get in here will get his head blowed off and I ain't foolin'.'

A man's voice yelled: 'You're being a fool, Cassidy. We'll be back. You can't keep a sharp watch all night and when we do come, it'll be the worse for you.'

There was the sound of men moving around in the street. Clem guessed that the demonstrators were dispersing, moving off, possibly back to the saloons or the hotel.

He doubted if any of them would be returning to their homes. They were determined on a hanging and nothing was going to stop them. Sooner or later, and certainly before daybreak, they would come back, and when they did, he did not think the six men in the outer office would be able to hold them.

A minute later, Cassidy came along the passage, holding the lantern and his rifle. 'Seems you two have stirred up a mite of trouble in town,' he said thinly. 'That crowd is pretty riled up about you for some reason.'

'They're being stirred up by a handful of troublemakers,' Clem said tightly. 'They know that we aren't in with the rustlers and that when the sheriff gets back he can prove our innocence, so they have to string us up before he can return.'

The other hesitated. 'They'll come again,' he said dubiously.

'Don't you reckon that we should have a chance to defend ourselves if they do?'

'Now you know I can't give you back your guns,' said the other quickly. 'But you got no call to worry. If they do come, they'll get the same as they got a little while ago.'

'When they come again, they'll be ready for that. You seriously think that six men can hold off that crowd?'

'That's our job,' said the other stiffly. He looked down at the gun in his hand. Then he turned and stumped off along the passage. As a parting shot, he said: 'I'll be glad when I do get you off my hands, rustlers or not.'

Outside, in the street, silence seemed to press down more tightly than before.

CHAPTER FOUR

LYNCHING PARTY!

Midnight; and there was still silence in the streets of Bitter Ridge. But it was not an easy silence. The town was not asleep, although it gave the semblance of slumber to the men seated in the small cell at the rear of the sheriffs office. Clem felt the weariness grow in him, knew that it had been a long time since he had slept undisturbed for a whole night. But there would be no sleep for him or Doc that night, not with a lynching party somewhere out there in the darkness, biding its time, waiting until they judged the moment for action to be opportune. Then they would move in on the jail and this time they would not be sent running back with their tails between their legs as they had been earlier. This time they would come with guns and not even the deputies would stand in their way.

Standing by the window, Clem stared out into the cool darkness of the night. There was a riot of half-formed thoughts and ideas racing through his mind. Desperately he searched his memory for some picture of that tall, black-bearded man who seemed so desperately intent on killing them. Had he ever met that man before? Had he been a man Clem and Doc had hunted down and caught

73

in the past? There wasn't a solitary memory in his mind of the other and he turned his thoughts to Goudie. Where was the killer now? Still back there in the desert? Or had he proved too clever for them, had that false trail he had laid to the south enabled him to double back, not into Bitter Ridge where they had expected him to show up, but back to Twin Buttes? It was a certainty that he would be safe back there in that lawless town, possibly even safer than here in Bitter Ridge.

Tightening his grip on the bars that laced up and down across the narrow window, he tried to pick out the faintest sound that would warn him of the coming of the lynch mob. But the town lay quiet under the stars. A coyote howled thinly in the far distance, many miles beyond the outer fringe of the town, the sound carrying easily in the clear air.

Where was Sheriff Howell now? Had he reached the Cawdrey place, discovered for himself that they had been telling the truth, and was he at that moment, racing his mount back to town in an attempt to save the lives of two innocent men, probably knowing that there would be a lynch mob around in town, taking every advantage of his absence to force over their own kind of law.

Behind him, on the bunk, Doc Foran stirred, rolled over and swung his legs to the floor. He got to his feet and walked over to the window, looking out at the stars.

'I must say I never thought the time would come when I would be locked away in some jail like this, on a charge of cattle thieving,' he said in a low, soft voice. 'Funny the way life turns about on itself and gets to a point where it doesn't seem to make any sense at all.'

'If Howell gets back in time, we'll be all right,' said Clem.

'And if he doesn't? I don't know about you, but I'm not very partial to having my neck stretched.'

'I'm wondering where they are now. It sounds pretty quiet out there, too quiet for my liking.'

'I'm wonderin' if those deputies are still awake through there. Maybe that's all that crowd is waiting for, to get them asleep. Then it won't be difficult for them to drag us out and string us up.'

Clem ran a dry tongue over equally dry lips. The silence seemed to grow more intense with every passing mood, until it screamed on his nerves more loudly than any sound. He pulled himself away from the window and forced himself to relax. His nerves and muscles were all tensed, his limbs stiff and painful.

Slowly, the minutes lengthened into hours. Still there was no sign that the townsfolk of Bitter Ridge intended to fulfil their threat and march on the jail once more. Doc rolled himself another smoke, lit it and sat back on the bunk, drawing deeply on the cigarette, grimacing as the smoke touched his dry throat. Outwardly, he seemed relaxed, but Clem knew that inside, he would be just as tensed and taut as he was.

A little after three o'clock in the morning, there was the sound of the far door opening and one of the deputies came along the passage, peered into the cell. 'You two all right in there?' he said thinly.

'Sure,' growled Doc Foran harshly. 'You reckon we'd have gone some place, with that lynch mob waiting outside for us in the street?'

'They seem to have dispersed quietly,' said the other. 'We don't figure they'll make any more trouble tonight.'

'You sure about that?' Clem did not like the complacency in the other's tone. Maybe this was what the crowd was banking on. As the hours went by and nothing happened, they would grow more lax inside the office, would not keep as close a watch on the street as before. That was when the danger would be at its highest.

'They know what happened the last time. A load of buckshot and they took off like a pack of startled rabbits.'

'Could be that the next time they'll have shotguns and you'll be on the wrong end of 'em,' grunted Doc forcibly.

'Once they've sobered up, they'll realize what fools they've been to listen to the trouble-makers and they'll have no more of it.'

He made his way back to the office, satisfied that everything was under control. Clem felt his hands tighten by his sides in impotent fury. How could anyone be so blind? he thought fiercely. Blindly believing that men like this would give up so easily. He glanced up at the window. The stars were still shining as brightly as before and the night was still as dark, with a cold wind blowing down the alley from the north.

Another hour, he thought dully, then the crowd would make their move. Now they would probably be still inside the saloon, talking things over in low voices. There would be no more singing. It wasn't likely that they would try to shoot them down inside the cell by stealth. They had tried that before and it hadn't worked. Besides, Clem had the feeling that the crowd wanted to see them strung up now, they firmly believed that he and Doc had ridden with the Texas Dusters, were members of that notorious outlaw band. Nothing was going to satisfy them now but to lynch them before the sheriff got back and insisted that everything be done legally.

Then, when the tension outside seemed to have become intolerable, they heard it. Faint at first, but growing louder, it was the unmistakable sound of men, heading along the main street. This time, they came on in silence. There was no shouting and talking.

A shotgun sounded from close by and Cassidy's voice yelled: 'All right, Ben, that's far enough. Another step and we'll open up on you.'

'You're going to shoot down honest and decent citizens of this town just to protect those lying, thieving rustlers?'

'Honest decent men don't come and try to take the law into their own hands,' called the other.

'We've waited a long time to get some of those rustlers,' came the reply. 'Now that we've got 'em we mean to make sure they don't do any more thieving, any more killing.'

Shots rang out, drowning his words. A shotgun blasted again, a tremendous sound. Then there was the noise of splintering wood, of voices yelling harshly. A window smashed and more gunfire broke out, a sporadic rattle that seemed to ring all the way along the street.

Doc edged his way towards the door of the cell, opened his mouth to yell at the deputies, but before he could let loose a single word, the crash of a door being busted off its hinges reached them and Clem knew that the crowd had poured into the outer office.

'Now just stay right where you are, Cassidy,' shouted a harsh voice. 'We don't want to harm you. But we do mean to have those two killers out of that cell.'

Booted heels sounded along the passage. There came the flickering yellow glow from a lantern and several shadows thrown along the walls by the light. Ten seconds later, there was a group of dimly seen shadows outside the cell, staring in.

'All right, you two,' yelled a gruff voice. A key turned in the lock and the door was thrust open on squealing hinges. 'Get outside.'

Clem moved forward. Doc got to his feet but apparently not quickly enough for Haswell. He swung the gun in his right hand and the top of the barrel and the foresight caught Doc on the side of the face, tearing across the skin. A trickle of blood dripped down the right cheek and fell from his chin on to his shirt.

They were led along the passage and into the outer

77

office. The deputies were lined up against one wall. Two of them were lying on the floor, evidently dead or unconscious.

'We got 'em, boys,' said Haswell tightly. He looked around at the deputies, fixing his gaze on Cassidy. 'You've been pretty stupid trying to stop us. We could've killed you for standing in our way like this. But we only want these two.'

'You'll never get away with taking the law into your own hands, Haswell,' said Cassidy. He eyed the other sharply. 'Once Sheriff Howell gets back, he'll want the answers to some questions and you'll find yourself arrested on a charge of murder.'

Haswell's eyes glittered with a feral hate. 'They didn't think of that when they shot down Clements and the other herders. If Howell doesn't intend to do anything, then we'll have to do it ourselves. But there's no time for talking. We've wasted enough time with that already.' He turned to three of the men with him. 'Better lock these men up in one of the cells where they can't interfere with our plans.'

'What about those two?' One of the men pointed to the unconscious figures on the floor.

'Take them too. They may come round and free the others.'

The two unconscious men were picked up and carried roughly out of the office and back along the corridor. Cassidy and the other three deputies were forced along at gunpoint. As he brushed past him, Clem glanced up at Cassidly, locked his gaze with his. Bitterly, he said: 'It seems that there's no place here for law and order.'

'Shut your mouth, killer,' snarled Haswell. He prodded the barrel of the gun deep into Clem's stomach, grinned viciously at the expression of pain that flashed over the other's features. 'Don't make me kill you before it's time,' he said thinly. 'I want to see you dangling from the end of a rope. I've waited a long time for this.'

'How do you know that you ain't making a big mistake,' muttered Clem. 'You ain't seen either of us before and you know it. Why jump to the conclusion that we're rustlers?'

'We've talked this over and we know,' said the other hoarsely. 'Ain't no point in trying to argue your way out of this.'

'And what do you figure on doing in the morning when the sheriff gets back with the news that we're not rustlers?' inquired Doc Foran.

'That ain't likely. All he'll want to do is keep you locked up there in jail until Judge Parkins gets here in a couple of months' time. But we ain't feeding a couple of men like you all that time and then have you slip through our fingers if they decide to take you out by stage. We'll finish this ourselves.' His eyes peered out at Clem under the bushy eyebrows, filled with a savage antagonism.

Outside, in the dark street, their horses were waiting. Someone had evidently fetched them from the livery stables.

'All right, saddle up,' ordered Haswell. He held the gun on them as they went forward. Several of the men climbed into the saddle, sat their mounts expectantly, eyes and faces hard as they stared at Clem and Doc. Wearily, Clem pulled himself up into the saddle, sat there, staring out at the others. They were ringed round now and it would be impossible for them to escape. They would be shot in the back before their mounts were able to clear the crowd. Although it was still early, there was a faint brightening in the east where the dawn was struggling over the horizon. It still wanted two hours to sun-up, but soon there would be enough light for these men to see by, sufficient light to throw a couple of riatas over the branch of a nearby tree, place the nooses around their necks and then slap their mounts from under them. 'Are we all ready?' called Haswell. He turned in his saddle and looked about him. The men nodded.

'Then let's get this finished with. The sheriff might get back here at any moment and I want these two strung up before he comes.'

'You seem in an almighty hurry to have us hanged,' Clem said loudly, so that everybody in the street might hear his words. 'Could it be that you've got some reason for making up these lies against us? You seem to be the one who's doing all of the talking here, giving all of the orders.' He turned his head and let his gaze wander over the faces of the other men there. 'What are you all doing, letting him boss you around like this? Reckon he might be in with the rustlers himself and he wants to throw the blame on somebody else so he picks on a couple of strangers who've just ridden into town and—'

'Keep your mouth shut.' While he had been speaking Haswell had edged his mount closer to Clem and his right fist, tightly-bunched, lashed out and caught him savagely on the side of the head, half knocking him out of the saddle. Desperately, Clem fought to retain a hold on his buckling consciousness. The other's hammer blow had almost knocked him out and there was a dull ringing in his ears as he forced air down into his heaving lungs and blinked his eyes in an effort to clear his vision.

'Now let's ride and finish the job,' ordered Haswell. He reached forward to grab the reins of Clem's horse, then paused as one of the men in the crowd spoke up. 'Just a minute, Ben. Let's hear what this man has to say first. It sounded mighty interesting to me just then.'

Haswell swung on the other, his eyes glittering. His right hand rested on his hip, very close to the butt of the gun he had pushed back into its holster.

'What's that?' he demanded.

'You heard what I said, Ben. I'd like to hear their side of the story. There will be plenty of time to stretch their necks before Howell gets back. It's more than a ten hour ride there and back to the Cawdrey place.'

Haswell slitted his eyes savagely. 'We ain't going to lose any more time. Now that's final. We talked this over carefully in the saloon and we were all agreed then that they're in with that bunch of outlaws. What's made you change your mind so suddenly?'

'Just that what he says has a ring of truth about it. Now that I come to remember what happened in the saloon it does seem that you were the one who did all of the talking and gave the orders. I don't recollect anybody else having anything at all to say. We listened to you, now we ought to listen to their side of the story.'

'Now see here, Webber—' snarled Haswell harshly. 'I thought I'd warned you that—'

He broke off as Clem said loudly. 'You see, he knows that if you hear what we have to say, you'll realize that maybe Sheriff Howell was right, maybe we have been wrongly accused of this and that Haswell here has something else on his mind when he wants us to be strung up so quickly.'

Again the heavy fist hammered at Clem's head, but this time he had anticipated it and managed to jerk his head back a little so that the hard knuckles merely grazed along his ear. But there was still enough force in the blow to send him reeling sideways in the saddle and he only managed to maintain his balance with difficulty.

There was a change in the crowd's mood now. Clem sensed it and he knew that Haswell had too, knew that unless he took things carefully, the crowd could go against him. Forcing himself upright, Haswell growled. 'What is it you want to say, killer?'

'Only that Sheriff Howell has ridden out to the Cawdrey

ranch to prove that we aren't with the Texas Dusters. Cawdrey's range was attacked last night and a thousand head or so stolen. We saw the thieves ride 'em off but there wasn't anything two men could do against that bunch.'

Haswell laughed harshly. 'I'll say not. You wouldn't want to shoot down your own kind.'

'Cawdrey can testify that he found us on his land trying to help those men who had been shot down in the raid.'

'You're lying,' snapped Haswell. He turned to the ring of men. 'They're just trying to blind you. What else would you expect them to say when there's the prospect of the rope waiting for 'em?'

'Reckon Haswell's right,' growled a man at the back of the crowd. 'I say we ought to take 'em out of town and string 'em up right now.'

One of Haswell's trouble-makers, placed there deliberately to sway the crowd in case something like this happened, thought Clem. He tightened his lips.

Another man spoke up in the same vein from a different direction. Even Clem felt a grudging admiration at the way the other had handled things, had made these preparations for every possible circumstance that was likely to arise. The other was making sure that the mood of the crowd swayed back in his favour. There were faint murmurs from more men at the back. Clem let his gaze follow the sounds.

There was no pity there, no belief on their faces. More of Haswell's men, he guessed. Even if the crowd refused to go with him on this, Haswell probably had enough of his own there to carry it off.

'You got anything more to say?' Haswell turned and glared at him, his fingers curling around the butt of his Colt.

Clem tightened his lips, knew that he had made his play and lost. 'That's what I figured,' grinned the other. He nodded to the crowd. 'Then let's go. You got the riatas?'

A man rode out of the crowd and held his arm high, the new ropes clenched in his fist as he lifted them over his head. A great cry came up from the crowd. Haswell had them now. They were nearly all with him. Only the man who had spoken up for them, Clem noticed, looked dubious, as though he was not entirely satisfied with what was happening, but in spite of this, he wheeled his mount and rode with the others as they made their way along the street, their horses hemming Clem and Doc Foran in, so that there was no possibility of them even attempting to make a getaway.

On either side of the main street, the buildings were in darkness. Silence seemed to lie over the town and there was only the sound of the steady hoofbeats of their horses as they walked them to the edge of town.

At the end of the main street, they paused as Haswell held up his hand. He seemed to be listening for something, his head a little on one side, then he nodded tersely and motioned them on again. Now they were out of town, moving into the rough country that lay beyond. Clem narrowed his eyes, trying to make out details of their surroundings. The pale light of the greying dawn at their backs, picked out the tall, rising mounds of rock on either side of the trail, as it twisted among them and in the distance, he could make out the long, low ridge which gave the town its name.

They rode in slow silence for perhaps a quarter of an hour, taking their time. Haswell seemed content to move the horses at a walking pace now that they were out of town. Clearly, he did not expect any trouble here. Directly ahead of them was a small clump of trees and Haswell pointed as they came into view.

'That looks like the best place for a hanging,' he said and there was an icy calm in his tone. 'Throw those ropes over the branch and we'll finish it.'

The man with the riatas rode forward, gigging his mount until he came beneath the out-thrusting branch that hung over the trail at that point. He tossed one of the ropes neatly over it, then pulled on it with all of his strength, making certain that the branch would take the strain of a man's weight jerking on the end of a rope. He looked round finally, satisfied.

'This ought to do,' he agreed.

He threw the other rope over so that the nooses hung down from the trees, swaying gently in the cold breeze that sighed along the trail.

'Tie their hands behind their backs,' snapped Haswell.

Two men moved out of the waiting crowd. Clem's arms were grabbed and placed roughly behind his back while the rope was lashed around his wrists, cutting deeply into the flesh as the man drew it tight.

'Reckon that ought to hold long enough,' he said, uttering a harsh laugh. He stepped away, nodded to Haswell.

'Good. Then hang them.' It was simply said and there was no argument. Clem sat tight in the saddle as his horse was led forward until it stood directly beneath the tree. One of the men drifted forward, reached out and placed the noose around his neck, then stepped back, looked inquiring at Haswell, before turning towards Doc Foran.

Haswell gave a faintly amused chuckle. 'Leave the other one. We'll hang 'em one at a time. It ought to give the Doc a chance to see what is in store for him.'

The utter callousness in his voice sent a wave of shock through Clem. He tightened his arms by his sides, swallowed thickly and pushed his gaze to one side, staring at Doc Foran. The other's face was tight, almost unrecognizable.

'You got anything to say before you hang, Winters?'

muttered Haswell. He drove his horse forward until he was beside Clem.

'Only that sooner or later, the law is going to catch up with you and then you'll find yourself on the end of a rope. Maybe I'll not be here to see it, but it'll come.'

Haswell grinned, his teeth showing in the shadow of his face. 'You're wrong, Winters. We know who we've got here. This is the law of this state, we hang cattle thieves and killers.'

'You've got no proof that we're either,' grunted Doc harshly. 'And the same goes for the sheep who've followed you out here. They don't have any minds of their own and you planted your men in the crowd so that they could sway the vote for you back there outside the sheriff's office.'

'You won't do any good talking like that,' snarled the other. He moved his horse a few feet away and sat tight and expectant in the saddle, lips thinned back across his teeth.

Clem braced himself. The rope was rough on his flesh, still loose, but ready to tighten in the instant that his mount leapt from beneath him as Haswell lashed it with his quirt. He sucked in a deep breath, held himself tight. Behind him, he heard Haswell move, suck in his own breath as he lifted the quirt.

A man coughed nervously close by. Then, almost before Clem was aware of it a rifle shot rang out. He flinched instinctively expecting the hammer of that bullet into his flesh. Then he almost slumped forward in the saddle as the pull on the rope slackened.

A harsh voice said: 'I figured you might try to do something like this, Haswell. Now stand away from there before I put the next bullet into you.'

With an effort Clem lifted his head and forced himself to focus his eyes on the man who sat his mount easily, a few yards away by the side of the trail, the smoking rifle in his hands swinging a little to cover the bunch of men.

Sheriff Howell had come up so quietly from the rocks that no one had heard his silent approach. Now he sat watching them, his gaze flicking from one man to the other. Then he said: 'You all right, Winters?'

Clem nodded. 'You got here just in time, Sheriff,' he said harshly. 'Another five seconds and it would have been too late.'

He rubbed his neck after one of the men, prompted forward by Howell, cut the rope that bound his wrists. His skin was chafed by the rope. Doc Foran edged towards him, gripped him tightly by the arm.

A moment later another group of men swung up out of the shadows that ran along the side of the trail. Through blurred vision, Clem recognized Cawdrey and some of his hands. They sat in a tight circle facing the men from Bitter Ridge, waiting for any sign of trouble. Swinging slowly in his saddle, sucking the cool, refreshing air down into his heaving lungs, Clem knew that there would be no trouble. These men would never dare to go against Cawdrey and his hands, even if Howell had not been holding that rifle on them.

'We figured that the time for talking was past,' growled Haswell.

'So I see.' There was a biting anger in the sheriff's voice. 'I ought to string you up there, Haswell.'

'We don't like cattle thieves in Bitter Ridge.' The other spoke defiantly, defensively.

'These men are not cattle thieves.' Cawdrey spoke up at that, gigging his mount forward. 'These men came here from Twin Buttes. I offered them jobs on my spread but they said they had business in Bitter Ridge.' His hard gaze fell on the men in front of him. 'Somehow, I doubt if it was this kind of business.'

*

Dawn came on, lingered briefly, then turned into full daylight as the sun came up. On the low bed in the hotel room, Clem turned over as the sunlight fell full on his face, shining into his eyes. He got up, dressed, rubbed his throat tenderly for a moment, then went on down into the dining-room. Doc was already there at the table.

'Why do you figure the sheriff asked us to meet him at his office this morning?' Doc asked, as Clem sat down and ordered sowbelly and coffee.

'No idea. Expect he has some reason. Probably to do with what happened yesterday. Could be that he wants to apologize on behalf of the town for the fact that the decent, honest citizens almost murdered us.'

Clem ate slowly and thoroughly when the food was set before him. Outside, the town seemed to have a different air about it. The sun threw long shadows across the dusty street. A couple of trail riders moved by at an easy lope. Doc waited until he had finished his meal, then got to his feet. 'Reckon we'd better go over and see what the sheriff has on his mind. We don't want to keep him waiting. Not after he saved your life this morning.'

'Sure,' Clem said. He rose and followed the other out into the street. Slowly, they made their way over to the sheriffs office. Howell was seated in the chair behind the desk, got to his feet as they entered.

'I'm sure glad I managed to get back in time this morning to stop that lynching,' he murmured, nodding towards the chairs. 'I've got a favour to ask of you both.'

'Sure, go ahead.'

Howell swung away to stare through the window. 'We know why you came here and about this man you've been trailing since you left Twin Buttes. I can't say I like bounty hunters, but at least it proves you aren't in with the Texas Dusters and I figure you as men who are fast with a gun. I want you to help us track down this band of cattle thieves.'

'How do you know that we're bounty hunters?' asked Doc.

'You're not green,' Howell said cautiously. 'You've had a lot of experience and I figure that maybe it's the kind of experience we need.'

Clem said: 'How do you figure we can help you round up this bunch when you and your posses who obviously know this country well have failed?'

Howell looked at him, something half formed on his thin lips. Clem saw caution hold the other back and thought to himself: He still isn't too sure of us, even now.

Before the sheriff could say anything further, the street door swung open and Cawdrey came in. His silver hair showed long from under his hat as he closed the door carefully behind him, then pulled down the green shade. 'Better not to take too many chances on being seen,' he muttered. Turning to face Clem and Doc, he went on: 'Has Howell put our proposition over to you yet?'

'I was just on the point of sounding them out, Tracy,' broke in the sheriff. 'Maybe you had better tell 'em.'

Cawdrey lowered himself into a chair, thrust his legs out in front of him. Hunting in his shirt pocket, he brought out a black cigar, bit off the end, then put it into his mouth and lit it, eyes still fixed on Doc and Clem.

'You must think a lot about catching up with this man Goudie,' he said, shooting a quick look, filled with suspicion. 'I've known a few bounty hunters in my time and they would never think of hunting a man across fifty miles of the worst kind of territory in the country, over those burning alkali flats, unless they had a real good reason.' He breathed deeply on his cigar.

'There's the reward out for him – dead or alive,' put in Doc.

'No,' said Cawdrey, soft and final. 'It's not that easy.' His eyes gave them a careful study. 'They never heard of

88

Goudie back in Twin Buttes, I checked with the sheriff there. But they have heard of him down in Tucson. Shot up a couple of stages, got away with about a thousand dollars, killed a stage guard and one of the passengers, shot them both down in cold blood even when he had the draw on them.'

'You seem to know a hell of a lot about him,' said Clem quietly. He tried to gauge the other's interest, to judge what was in this man, what lay at the back of all his talk.

'I know that there's only five hundred dollars on Goudie's head if you do bring him in,' said the rancher. His smile was a white streak against the shadows of his serious face. 'That makes me think. No man is going to trail a killer all this way, through that desert out there, for that kind of reward.' He smoked his cigar for a long moment and the silence grew in the room, long and almost accusing. Out of the corner of his eye, Clem threw a quick glance at Howell, wondering how he went along with this. The tight look on the sheriff's face accentuated the planes and hollows of his features, making them seem more bony and rugged than usual. His eyes narrowed on Clem in appraisal and then widened.

'All right,' said Clem suddenly, breaking the clinging silence which had built up around him. 'What do you figure we are?'

Cawdrey listened to his voice and weighed it carefully. He seemed to have started out cool and suspicious of them and looked as if he was anxious to keep it that way. Still, Clem saw the change in the rancher's lips and he saw the small gust of expression flicker over his face.

'Either we have all misjudged you both and you are members of that rustling gang, which I very much doubt – or you're a couple of lawmen, probably rangers.'

Clem smiled thinly. 'And if we're lawmen? What do you propose to do then?'

'Then I'm quite sure that we can turn our individual interests to a mutual advantage.'

'How's that?'

'We want to smash this gang and you want Goudie.' He pulled deeply on his cigar until the end glowed red, then let the grey ash fall to the floor. 'Goudie is with them right now. I suppose you guessed he might be when he didn't come riding into town.'

Clem hardened his lips, pressing them into a tight line. 'You're sure of that? Or is this just a trick to get us to join you?'

'We're sure.' He nodded and Clem knew instinctively that the other was telling the truth. 'There isn't much that we don't know about strangers that come riding into these hills, particularly if they come from the desert out east. Every rancher in the territory has lost cattle to the Dusters. Now we've banded together in an attempt to stamp them out.'

'Yet in spite of that you still need us to help you,' put in Doc Foran. 'Why?'

'That's easily explained. We'll use any man we can to smash this outfit.' He eyed Clem shrewdly, then switched his gaze to Doc. 'Don't worry about your identity being spread all over town. Most of the folk still feel that you're in league with these *hombres* and we want 'em to go on thinking that – for a while at least.' Cawdrey pushed himself up, sat straighter in his chair. He had a great assurance about him, he had no real doubt about himself.

'We know that somebody here in town is passing word to them about any plans that we make. Until we know who that somebody is and how he's doing it, they'll go on taking our cattle in comparative safety, stealing them from under our very noses, riding them off into the hills when we least expect it. Nobody has enough men to guard each herd sufficiently. There are too many in the gang for that.'

Clem nodded. He could readily see the other's problem. Now, though, he and Doc had one of their own. Now that they knew for sure that Goudie had lined himself up with the rustlers, it meant they would not find it easy to pry him loose from the hills. The only chance they had was to throw in their lot with these men, hoping that they might thus get their chance to catch up with the killer they were trailing.

'You got any plans in mind?'

Cawdrey shook his head slowly. 'None that we ain't tried out before, with no luck.'

'What do you know about this man Haswell? He seemed mighty anxious to get us hanged last night, stirring up that lynch mob in the saloon, even coming with two of his men to try to gun us down in the cells. Seems to me it was more than just a desire to get rid of two men he thought were in cahoots with those rustlers, even when he didn't have any proof at all about us.'

'Haswell?' Sheriff Howell looked up in mild surprise. 'He owns the store along the street a piece. Also runs the telegraph office from there. Nothing against him so far, except for what he tried to do during the night. A bit impatient, I guess, but that's all. Unless you want to sign out a warrant against him?'

'No, nothing like that. Do you reckon he could be in league with the Texas Dusters?'

Howell watched him with sharp eyes, filled with curiosity. 'Why do you suggest that? Any reason?'

'Seems to me that, as well as you, he might have guessed who we really are, and he wanted to get rid of us quickly before we could start probing and asking awkward questions, making trouble for him. I've tried to recall his face but I don't recollect having bumped into him anywhere before.'

'If he had ridden out of town to warn them of our plans, we would have known,' asserted the sheriff positively.

'You're sure that you can keep a watch on every man who rides out of town?'

'Mebbe not. But if it is Haswell, then he can only go at night. You can't leave a telegraph office unattended during the day without somebody noticing that you're gone.'

'No, could be that you're right and I'm going off along the wrong trail about him.' Clem gave a brisk nod. Inwardly, he still felt that there was some connection, but he failed to see it and without any real proof it would count very little with these men. But he was determined to keep a close watch on the big, black-bearded man. 'How do you figure we can help you?'

'Stick around in town for a while. Don't act suspicious but try to find out as much as you can. If you're right about Haswell, he may try to do something, so keep your eyes open as well as your ears. If you do find anything, let the sheriff or me know. We'll take it from there.'

'I gather that if there is to be a showdown, we both get in on the deal,' broke in Doc, turning away from his position at the window. With a harsh grin, he went on 'We still want this man Goudie you say is mixed up with them.'

'You'll have him,' promised Cawdrey. 'Me and my boys will be riding out of town before noon. Perhaps one of you might like to ride with us, see if it's possible to trail the herd out into the desert, where you noticed it when you were camping there.'

'Sure,' Doc nodded. 'If there is a trail there, reckon I ought to be able to find it.'

'Good.' Cawdrey got to his feet, flicked the end of the cigar into the empty fireplace. 'We'll be riding out in three hours or so. I hope you have better luck than we have tracking them down. Seems impossible that an entire herd of a thousand head can vanish into thin air like that, without leaving any tell-tale tracks for us to follow.'

He went to the door, raised the shade, glanced quickly up and down the street and then stepped outside, along the boardwalk, and then down into the dusty street.

CHAPTER FIVE

A TRAP IS LAID

Clem sat at the corner table of the saloon, with his back to the wall, where he could see everyone who came in. There were four men playing stud at a nearby table and several others at the bar. In the far corner, a small, hook-nosed man in a striped shirt played idly at the piano, his hat tilted far back on his head staring almost dreamily in front of him as his fingers moved over the ivory keys.

All of that day, he had drifted around town, trying to pick up something that would tell him whether there was anyone who could get hold of the necessary information and pass it on to the men in the hills without arousing too much suspicion. So far he had discovered nothing. Doc had ridden out with Cawdrey and his men at noon and had not returned.

He sipped the whiskey in his glass, refilled it from the bottle on the table in front of him. He had caught a brief glimpse of the black-bearded Haswell during the day. In spite of the fact that the man had done nothing in the least suspicious, Clem still figured him to be a key man in the trouble.

Glancing up over the rim of the glass he noticed the

94

man who came in through the batwing doors, looking about him for a moment before his gaze fell on Clem. He came walking right over straight towards Clem's table. For a moment, he failed to remember where he had last seen the other although the man's face was familiar. Then he recalled the man in the crowd who had argued and stood up to Haswell outside the sheriff's office after the mob had taken Doc and himself out of the jail and were hurrying them off to hang them.

The man eased his way among the rows of tables, then reached his own. His eyes swept around him for a moment, a trifle nervously, as if he realized that perhaps he ought not to be there, then he leaned forward a little and said in a low voice: 'Mind if I join you, Mister Winters?'

'Not at all.' Clem nodded to the other seat.

The man lowered himself into the chair. He kept his hands on the table, fingers drumming nervously for a moment, as if he were all tensed up inside, afraid of something that was riding him. From the other's hands, Clem guessed that he was not a gunfighter. Perhaps he had only ridden with the mob because he had been drunk and had been talked into it by the others, swayed against his better judgment by the persuasive power of Haswell's oratory.

'I feel that we all owe you and your partner an apology, Mister Winters,' he said harshly. He did not look up at Clem as he spoke, but continued to stare down at his fingers on the table in front of him.

'Forget it,' said Clem. He pushed the bottle towards the other. 'Have a drink and put it all down to bitter experience. Besides, if I remember rightly, I noticed you were the only one in the crowd who had the guts to stand up to Haswell.'

'Haswell, sure.' The other nodded quickly. There was a look of bitterness on his face. 'I felt sure it was all wrong, that you ought to have been given the chance of a proper trial. I don't know why we all listened to him as we did in the saloon.'

'Maybe the reason was because he was buying all of the drinks,' suggested Clem.

'That's right. He seemed so sure that you were both with this rustling outfit. He said that you were in town to find out about the guards on the herds and where they were, getting the news through to those men in the hills.'

'You known Haswell long?' Clem tried to sound casual.

'About a year, probably a little longer.'

'They tell me he runs a store here.'

'And the telegraph office. He's been here about a couple of years. Old Ben Rowles was here before him. Then he was retired and went back east, and we got Haswell.'

Clem watched as the other drank his whiskey at a single gulp, twisting his face into a grimace as the raw liquor hit the back of his throat on the way down. Lifting his glance, Clem stared over the other's shoulder as the saloon doors swung open. There was no mistaking Haswell as he came in. His narrowed gaze swept over everybody in the room, missing no one. It paused for the barest instant as it fell on Clem and the man with him, seemed to flicker briefly for a moment as if Haswell were trying to make up his mind about something then moved on.

For a minute he stood there just inside the doorway, thumbs hooked into the heavy gunbelt that he wore. Twin Colts, Clem noticed. Funny that a mere storekeeper should go around town armed like that. It certainly seemed to be in keeping with the man himself, but not with the job he did in town. The tick of suspicion grew again in his mind as the big man went over to the bar and stood with his elbows hooked on to it.

Clem's companion must have caught the sudden

change in his expression for he turned sharply in his seat, stared across the room at Haswell's broad back, then looked back. Urgently, he said in a hissed whisper: 'Don't start anything in here with Haswell, Mister Winters. He's got a lot of his friends spread around the room.'

'I don't aim to start any trouble.' Clem said tightly. 'In fact, I'll go over and have a drink with him.'

He pushed back his chair and walked slowly towards the bar. Several pairs of eyes followed him as he wove between the tables and he saw, by the sudden tensing of Haswell's shoulders that the other was aware of him.

Clem went up to the bar and stood beside the other. 'Whiskey,' he said to the bartender. 'And the same for my friend here.'

Haswell turned and there was a look of surprise on his hard features. For a moment, Clem had the impression that he meant to refuse. The man's eyes narrowed to mere slits and his brow furrowed as he evidently tried to think of some reason why Clem should be doing this. Then he forced himself to relax uttered a sharp, harsh laugh.

'Sure, I'll drink with you,' he said thickly. He turned his body so that he could see everyone in the saloon, resting his elbows behind him on the bar.

Clem picked up his drink and drank it slowly. He was acutely aware of the strained silence in the room. Even the four players at the far table had stopped their game and were glancing towards the bar as if expecting trouble to flare up at any moment.

'You got anything on your mind, Winters?' asked Haswell sharply. He lifted his glass, then tossed it back with a sudden gulp and set it back down on the bar.

'Not really,' Clem spoke quietly and casually. 'Should I have?'

'Seems to me you might be sore at what happened during the night.'

Just a mistake.' he shrugged. 'Anyone can make a mistake, I guess. And the town does seem to be pretty stirred up about these rustlers.'

Haswell was still surprised and suspicious, but he gave a slow nod, his eyes narrowed. 'I still figure you're somehow connected with those thieving coyotes up there in the hills.' He looked round at Clem and there was a challenge in his eyes, giving Clem a bright-black glance. 'But the sheriff and Tracy Cawdrey seem satisfied that you ain't, so who am I to argue?'

Clem finished his drink. He could see that Haswell was worried about something. The man's gaze kept flicking from one side of the saloon to the other, occasionally towards the doors as if expecting someone to come barging in, bringing trouble with them. Yes, that was it. All of a sudden, he guessed the cause of the other's concern. He was trying to figure out where Doc was. He had obviously missed the other, probably figuring that he was still somewhere around, uneasy in his mind until he located him.

Heavily, Haswell turned back to the bar. Evidently he considered that there was going to be no danger to him at the moment.

'They tell me that you were on the scene when those rustlers ran off Cawdrey's herd,' he said a moment later, without turning his head. 'How come you never took a shot at any of them if you were as close to the critters as they say you were?'

'No point in taking on more than twenty men.' Clem forced evenness into his tone. 'Besides it was none of our business. We don't get ourselves into anything unless we know what's going on. It ain't too healthy to do that.'

'Reckon a man can get 'himself into real trouble though, if he does that,' said the other. 'You rode into Bitter Ridge just after they pulled that raid. We figured you came on purpose. Somebody gets the information

98

through to them.'

Clem lifted his brows a little as a thought came to him. He said: 'I reckon I could tell quite a lot if I was in cahoots with them as you seem to think I am.'

'What sort of things,' Haswell's eyes narrowed suddenly.

Clem shrugged. 'You're forgetting that Cawdrey offered me a job on the spot after those two hands of his had been shot in the back. I figured on taking it. I'm to join one of the herds tomorrow out in the west pasture. Seems they got only a handful of men out there and Cawdrey is expecting some more trouble at any moment.'

'So he means to increase the riders on the big herd?' It was simply said and there was no inflection in the other's voice. He leaned his elbows heavily on the bar, resting the whole of his weight on them, stared off into the distance, apparently not caring whether Clem answered the question or not. But there was a little muscle jumping uncontrollably in his right cheek and Clem knew that he was holding himself with an effort.

'That's where you're wrong. He reckons they'll try for the smaller herd down in the south meadows this time. So he has as many men as he can spare hiding out in the rocks overlooking the valley. If the Dusters do try for the herd as he thinks they will, they'll be shot to pieces before they know they've been ambushed.' He deliberately kept his voice low, leaning forward conspiritorially. He saw the crafty gleam that came into Haswell's eyes but pretended not to notice.

'You seem to know a lot of what Cawdrey intends to do for a man who's only been in the territory for a few days.'

'Like you say, it could be because he knows that we're not cattle thieves.'

'Could be.' Haswell gave a brief nod. He poured himself another drink, then drank it down quickly before standing away from the bar. Then he gave a quick look around the saloon and moved towards the doors, pausing there for a second before stepping through into the street. The doors swung shut behind him. Clem paused to finish his drink, set the glass on the bar, then walked after him, pushing the doors open. Outside, it was dark. At the far end of the street a couple of horses moved, walking towards the saloon. Clem threw a swift glance along the street. He could just make out Haswell's dim figure moving along the boardwalk. The other did not seem to know that he was being watched, for he did not pause, nor did he turn his head to glance behind him.

Had he fallen for the trick? Clem wondered. If he had, then he would be on his way to pass on that information to someone in the rustling outfit and when he did that, Clem intended to be there at the time. He began to edge slowly and cautiously along the boardwalk in the darkness. There were the usual sounds of the town around him, forming a familiar background.

Haswell was still walking slowly along the boardwalk about fifty feet ahead of him. He stepped over one of the side streets, then cut along past the front of the stores, heading towards the edge of town. Clem waited until he had moved on, before stepping down on to the dust of the alley. He was almost too slow. A wild figure lunged out of the darkness to one side. Evidently the other had been crouching there waiting for him. One of Haswell's men. The thought flashed through his mind in the split second before the other reached him, one arm upraised. The dim light flashed bluely on the barrel of the gun that swung down in a descending arc towards his head. He was already turning instinctively as he glimpsed the other out of the corner of his eye, ducking swiftly under the blow. It caught him on the shoulder, a glancing impact that sent a searing stab of agony searing along his arm and into his body, numbing him. He lashed out sharply, felt the jar as his bunched fist connected on the other's chin, hurling him back against the wall of the building. He crashed against the wooden side and sagged to the ground, flailing out sideways as he went down, trying to clutch at something to prevent him from falling.

Turning, Clem glanced along the boardwalk. Haswell had paused at the sound, was standing there watching, peering into the darkness behind him. The man in the alley was struggling to get to his feet, sucking air down into his heaving lungs, thrusting himself forward. With a wild rush, he came in and Clem saw the killing fever in the man's eyes, distorting his face as he drew his lips back over his teeth. Clem knew that he would have to finish the man off before he could get after Haswell and he knew that Haswell had engineered this, had known he might follow him and had arranged for a reception committee to be waiting for him.

The man grabbed at his arm, tried to swing him round. For a moment, Clem was caught off balance by the very savagery of the other's move. His shoulder blades hammered against the wooden wall of the building, driving all the air out of his lungs. He hung there for a moment, fighting for breath, struggling to focus his eyes on the man in front of him, saw the grinning face looming against him, arm raised again. A blunt instrument crashed against the side of his face and the lights in the street danced in front of him as his head jiggled on his shoulders. There seemed to be fire in his cheek. He braced himself, swung hard at the other, saw the man weave his head back so that the blow merely grazed his chin, doing little damage. The other sensing that he had Clem at a disadvantage, came boring in, arms swinging now, landing blows to Clem's head.

With an effort, he kept his head moving, blocking as many of the wild blows as he could with his arms and elbows. He could hear the other's rasping breath, felt the blow of a heavy body striking him at an angle, the smell of alcohol in his nostrils. He shifted sideways, brought his right fist up from his boots and blasted a hard blow off the man's nose, felt it squash under his knuckles. The warm flow of blood burst over the other's face under the solid, jarring impact and he derived a feeling of pleasure from it. Another hammer blow caught his assailant on the jaw and neck, hurling him to one side. It had the effect of giving Clem a brief respite and he drew air down into his lungs, forcing his vision to clear. There was still a ringing in his ears but he could see properly now and the man's face no longer danced and wavered in front of his eyes.

There was the other rushing at him. Clem stepped back from the man's wild, bullish charge. The other telegraphed his wild swing and it was the simplest matter to step inside it and send two blows to the man's stomach. As he dropped forward under the impact of the blows, Clem drove a hard right to his chin. The man seemed to hang there for a moment, arms held outward in a grotesque posture, his head tipped back as if he were staring up at the stars, trying to draw down strength from them. Then every ounce of strength seemed to leave him, his knees buckled as if unable to bear his weight any longer and he toppled forward on to his face. His arms caught at Clem's feet as the other tried, even though unconscious, to take a tight hold on him to prevent himself from going all the way down.

Clem threw him a swift glance, tried to remain upright himself. He felt dizzy and there was still a sharp pain in the side of his face and down one side of his body where that first blow had hammered against his flesh. He looked about him swiftly, screwing up his eyes as he forced his vision to steady. The alley was deserted. Evidently no one had heard the fight, or if they had, they had concluded that it was wiser not to go and investigate.

He moved out into the main street. The cool air that blew along it soothed the pain in his face and he was able to stand upright and walk forward without staggering too .much. There was no sign of Haswell. He had expected that. If the assailant had not intended to kill him, he had at least been placed there to make certain that Clem did not follow Haswell too closely. In that he had undoubtedly succeeded.

Clem went out into the middle of the main street where he could see along both sides. Only at one end was there anyone in sight, two small men, neither of whom could have been Haswell. He hesitated. What to do now? Was there any place the other could have gone?

There was the possibility he had ridden out of town to some secret rendezvous in the hills. If that were so, then there would be no chance whatever of picking up and following his trail in the darkness. But there was another possibility. He cursed himself for not having thought of it before.

Turning on his heel, he hurried along the boardwalk. Back at the saloon, there was a noisy moment as a crowd of men came out, paused for a moment and then moved over to their mounts, climbing drunkenly into the saddle and riding out of town. Ahead of him there was a yellow light in the window of the small store kept by Haswell. A flickering, unsteady light that could come only from a lantern set on a table.

He crept forward with a soft tread, easing the gun in its holster.

Further along the street came a burst of noise and he edged to the window, flattening himself tightly against the side of the building. He paused there for a moment, before risking a quick glance inside. The lantern was standing on the wooden table at the far side of the room, its pale yellow glow falling on the shelves of supplies around the store. At first, he could see no sign of Haswell, but there was a strange tapping sound from inside the room that he couldn't place. Like a woodpecker hammering with its bill against the trunk of some giant tree.

Then, he caught sight of the other, half-hidden behind a pile of cartons. Haswell was crouched low over the desk, one hand on the key of the telegraph, the fingers moving up and down in the uneven rhythm as he sent the message flashing along the wires. So that was how the messages got out of Bitter Ridge to the rustlers. But it still not explain everything. Those lines went straight around the curve of the desert to the north, before they went into Twin Buttes and from there back east across the country. It was possible that there was someone in Twin Buttes receiving those messages and passing the information from there. He knew from experience that it was a particularly lawless town and anything might happen in the telegraph office there as it clearly did here.

Cautiously, he moved around the side of the building until he came upon the door at the rear. It opened off a small, evil-smelling alley. There was a garbage can standing beside it and as he twisted the handle and pushed, it opened under his weight. He felt a momentary surprise at this, then moved into the darkness inside the building. For a long moment, he paused there, letting his eyes become adjusted to the gloom. The room at the rear was stacked with boxes and he picked his way forward with extreme care. One wrong move here and he would give himself away to the other. The room smelled as if it had been abandoned for a long time, musty and dry and there was the remnant of odours that had been there for many years, collecting with time. He crossed the room in a blackness that was only slightly less absolute than that of the blackness of the night outside. He set one foot down before the other, testing the floorboards cautiously before he put his weight down on them.

There was a sudden scratching and a rat raced over the floor, scurried against the corner for an instant, then there was silence after the gritty sound. Letting his weight fall slow and easy, he found that in places there were no floorboards, only the hard-packed earth under his feet. He moved on until he came up against the far wall, reached out with his left hand and slid it slowly along the rough surface until it encountered the dull wooden surface of the door. He moved his fingers down in the darkness until they curled around the knob, rattling it slightly. It was only a small sound, but in the stillness and the confined space of that small room, it seemed to be magnified beyond all comprehension. He paused, holding his breath in his lungs until it hurt. Beyond the door, the staccato rattle of the telegraph key continued without hesitation and after a moment he relaxed and let his breath go in a slow gust.

Sightlessly, he explored the door, felt for the knob again and held it carefully, twisting it and pushing slightly. The door was not, as he had expected, locked. That simplified things considerably. He could smell the dust dragged up by his own feet, sharp in his nostrils, a dust that had lain there for years until it had become dried to a fine powder. Cautiously, he opened the door. A faint glimmer of yellow light seeped through around the narrow opening.

For a moment. there was silence, utter and complete in the house. Without waiting another second, he threw the door open and stepped inside, pausing there as his eyes grew accustomed to the yellow glow from the lamp. Haswell whirled swiftly, instinctively. A startled look came into his eyes and he started back from the telegraph key, his hands close to the guns at his waist.

Just try that move,' Clem warned, 'and it will be the last you'll make.'

'What do you reckon you're doing in here?' snarled the other. 'This is private property.'

'Maybe so,' Clem nodded his head slowly, keeping his gaze locked with the other's. 'But I had you figured all the time, Haswell. I guessed that you might be the link with these critters in the hills, but I needed proof. I'm not sure how you're getting it out to them at the other end, but I reckon that won't be too difficult to find out, once the sheriff hears of this.'

'I'm only sending out messages as I'm supposed to do.' The other still tried to bluff his way out of the situation. He kept his gaze on Clem. 'You forget that I'm the telegraph operator here.'

'I'm not forgetting anything,' muttered Clem tightly. 'Now step away from that key. If you want to try for those guns you're carrying, then you're at liberty to do so. That's your privilege.'

Haswell thinned his lips in a sneering smile. 'I reckon from the look of you that you're faster with a gun than I am. You seem to have had a lot more experience of that kind. I'd be a fool to go up against you, wouldn't I? You might even be able to claim that you shot me down in self-defence, when they find me here.'

'I've never shot a man in the back yet,' Clem said tightly. The emptiness of the building seemed to suffuse his voice so that there were faint echoes coming from the room leading off from the office. 'I'm taking you in to the sheriff. He can decide what to do with you.'

'And what proof have you got that I'm in league with these rustlers? Just because I'm here sending messages, something I'm paid to do?'

'That depends on the messages you're sending, doesn't it? It could be that you're warning your friends out there about the Cawdrey herd, when I told you in the saloon. The trouble is that it was all lies. It's the big herd that will

be closely guarded and when your friends act on the information that you've sent through to them, they'll not thank
you when we cut them down in the valley.'

'Why you—' The other lunged forward, hands dropping towards the guns in his belt. Then he froze there,
eyes starting from his head, his lips jutting out above the
black beard as the Colts were half drawn from Clem's
holsters and he knew that he was only a moment away
from death if he continued with his move. He sagged a
little, moved back a pace, leaned heavily against the desk,
apparently defeated, finished.

'That's better,' Clem muttered. 'Now come along.
Move!' He had the other in front of him, saw the growing
thought of action in Haswell's eyes again as he pushed
himself off the bar and took a step forward. He noticed
the instant hardening of the man's face, tightened his grip
on the butt of his guns.

Too late, Clem saw the piece of metal that the other
grasped in his left hand, something he had picked up
from the top of the desk as he had moved his hand away
from the transmitting key. It arced towards Clem's head as
the other brought his arm forward swiftly.

Clem had just time to jerk his head on one side, but
even so, the piece of jagged metal caught him just behind
the ear, knocking him sideways. He tried desperately to
catch himself from going down, from falling backward
against the chairs behind him, knowing that once he fell,
the other would pull his guns and squeeze the triggers.

His leg caught the edge of one of the chairs, and he
stumbled back, going down on to one knee, the Colts
jerked from their holsters in the same moment, barrels
lining up on Howell's chest as he sent his hands grabbing
downward, a grin of savage triumph on his broad face.
The guns were out of leather, swinging to cover Clem as he
forced himself upright.

A quick squeeze of the trigger and sound bucketed through the building, sending the echoes screaming along the other rooms. Haswell had fired without taking proper aim, too quickly and excitedly, and the bullet splintered into the chair within an inch of Clem's arm. Haswell loosed off another wild shot that ploughed a red-hot line along the muscles of Clem's upper arm so that he almost released his hold on the gun in his fist. He felt the warm slickness of blood soaking into the sleeve of his shirt. But a split second later, before the other could line up his guns again; he had fired. Haswell teetered on his toes as the bullet took him in the chest. He seemed to be standing on tiptoe as if trying to loom high over Clem, half-lying on the floor, his back pressed against the sharp edge of the chair.

Then he leaned loosely forward and kept on until he crashed down in front of the ranger, his head striking the floor with a dull and sickening thud. Slowly, breathing deeply to steady himself, Clem forced himself to his feet, pouched the gun and kept a tight hold with his other hand on the back of the chair as he stood, swaying a little, looking down at the man who lay on the floor between his feet.

Outside, the silence was broken by the sound of heavy footsteps running along the hollow-sounding boardwalks. They seemed to come from two directions and a moment later Clem picked out Howell's loud voice shouting above the rest. There came a quick knock on the door of the office and with an effort, he forced himself to go forward and unlock the outer door Howell stood there and there was a small crowd of men gathered at his back, looking excitedly past him into the dimly-lit room.

'What's happened here, Winters?' demanded the sheriff. He pushed his way past Clem, then stood and stared down at the figure of Haswell sprawled on the floor.

'I've suspected him for quite some time,' Clem said harshly. 'I figure he might be the one who's betraying you.'

Howell gave a quick look at him, then motioned to the deputy who stood inside the open doorway. 'Get the rest of those men away from here,' he ordered. 'There's no need for a doctor here.'

The crowd dispersed,, muttering among themselves. Going over to the door, Howell closed it, then turned back to face Clem. 'You're sure he's the one?' he asked harshly.

Clem nodded. 'He was in the saloon and I figured that if I could get him to think that I knew something of Cawdrey's plans for his herd, I might get him to give himself away. I warned him that Cawdrey had placed men to watch the smaller herd, but leaving the larger one relatively unguarded. I guessed that if he was the man we seek, he would waste no time to get that message to his friends in the hills.'

'So he came straight here.' Howell gave a quick nod. 'I ought to have guessed it before. The telegraph. One of the fastest ways of getting any information out of town.' He went over to the apparatus and stood looking down at it for a long moment, seemingly oblivious of the dead man lying on the floor near his feet.

Clem's hand moved slowly to his gun. He lifted it a little from its holster, easing it absently, and then pushed it carefully back into place. A moment passed. There was a movement out in the street.

'He'll have friends,' Clem said softly. 'I was warned there were some in the saloon. They may try to avenge his death.'

'Maybe.' Howell turned. 'But I reckon you'd better get out to Cawdrey's spread and warn him of what has happened here. Those rustlers know of that plan now and they'll attack the herd.'

Clem turned towards the door, then paused at a sudden commotion out in the street. There was the sound of a single horse coming fast from the north. He thrust open the door and stepped outside, peering along the darkness of the street until his eyes picked out the shape of the running horse and the man who lay low in the saddle, clinging around the animal's neck.

Clem recognized the horse instantly. He took three quick strides into the middle of the street, caught at the bridle as it lunged towards him, dragging him for a couple of yards before he finally succeeded in halting the animal. Carefully he eased Doc Foran from the saddle. There was blood on the other's shirt, holding it stickily against his flesh and he seemed barely conscious.

Sheriff Howell came running forward.

'He's been shot,' said Clem tightly. He laid the other on the ground and knelt beside him. The little man groaned and straightened out. Fresh blood from the wound had stained his shirt a bright red.

'Let's get him inside the saloon and I'll get Doc Barcroft,' muttered Howell. He motioned to some of the men, who picked up the wounded man and carried him carefully through the batwing doors of the saloon and stretched him out on one of the long tables. The man who had hurried off for the doctor came back a couple of minutes later with a tall, thin-faced man, dressed in black, who carried a small case with him. He set it down professionally on the table, then glanced up at Clem.

'How'd this happen?'

'We don't know.' Clem shook his head. 'His horse brought him back into town. He rode out with Tracy Cawdrey at noon.'

'He's lost a lot of blood, but fortunately the bullet hit him in the upper arm. It came clean out at the other side, so there's no need to probe for it.'

He washed the wound with sharp-smelling antiseptic, then bandaged it up. 'He'll be all right in a couple of days. He'll have a mighty stiff arm for a week or so though.

110

Won't be doing any gun-fighting.'

Doc moaned and opened his eyes, staring about him for a moment without any recognition in them. Then his gaze lowered until it caught Clem.

'They jumped me out on the trail down from the hills, Clem,' he said in a deep, husky whisper. 'Three of the varmints. I think I got one of them but I caught this slug and decided to head back for town. Must've passed out before I got here. Don't remember a thing.'

'You were nearly unconscious when we got you off your mount,' Clem said harshly. 'Did you recognize any of 'em?'

With an effort the other shook his head, winced a little as pain lanced through his ann. He glanced down at the bandages on it, looked towards Doctor Barcroft. 'You made a good job of that, Doctor,' he said softly. 'Doubt if I could have done a better job myself.'

The other merely sniffed and glanced away. 'He'll be all right once that wound heals,' he said stiffly. Turning, he stumped out of the saloon without a backward glance.

'I reckon you've hurt his feelings, Doc,' said Clem, grinning. 'But it shows that you'll soon be your old self again.'

'You don't think this is going to keep me on my back, do you?' grunted the other thickly. He tried to push himself on to his side, then fell back with the sweat beading his forehead as the effort told on him. 'Well, maybe a day or so, but then I'm going back into the hills and I sure hope I come up against those murderin' critters again, face to face this time, and not in the dark.'

'You might get that chance,' Clem told him. He straightened, got to his feet. 'But in the meantime, get back to the hotel and rest up until I get back.'

'Move easy if you're thinking of heading into the hills. There seem to be a lot of riders heading out there now. Trouble brewing, I feel certain.'

'I'll watch my step,' Clem promised. 'Now you get some rest. You've done enough for one day. The sheriff will fill you in on the details when I'm gone. Things have been happening here in town while you've been away.'

He walked towards the doors, pushed them open with the flat of his hand and stepped out into the street, watchful and wary now. Haswell would have friends in town, watching him now. If they saw him ride out, it was on the cards that they might decide to follow him.

CHAPTER SIX

THE TEXAS DUSTERS

The slim yellow crescent of a moon swung low on the western horizon as Clem Winters rode out of Bitter Ridge and cut along the narrow trail that led out in the rocky country. This was the trail he had been forced to ride. that night when Haswell and the other citizens of the town had busted Doc and himself from the jail and moved them out of town to string them up. He stayed with the main trail until he reached the very spot where the branch of a tree overhung the road. Then he swung off to the east, heading over rough, stony ground which lifted on an upgrade all the time, climbing to the hills. He knew that it would be almost dawn before he reached the Cawdrey ranch, but he felt little concern at that. The rustlers, even though they would have received Haswell's last message by now and might have already decided to act on it, would not ride out to attack that herd until the following night at the earliest.

They could not be certain that it wasn't a trap and they would probably scout the area first before launching their lightning raid. This time, however, if luck remained with

the ranchers, the raiders would find themselves unpleas-
antly surprised by the warm welcome they received when
they rode in for the kill.

Riding, he felt a wave of savage anger stir within him.
The knowledge that it had been these killers who had shot
down. Doc, brought the blood pounding into his temples.
Tightening his grip on the reins, he crouched low over the
neck of the horse as he rode into a wide thicket, the slim,
but wiry branches slashing at his face and neck as he
pushed through them. He felt reasonably confident that
no one from town would be able to follow his trail through
this rough country, no matter how good they believed
themselves to be. Once he paused, reining his mount on
the top of a long, high outcrop of smooth lava rock, straining his ears in an attempt to pick out any sound of pursuit.
But there was no sound behind him in the direction of the
town, although directly ahead of him he thought he could
hear the dim, tell-tale sound of riders on the move, cutting
diagonally across the path he was taking.

He listened for a repetition once the sound had died
away to a final starved echo in the distance. But there was
nothing more and he raked spurs across the horse's flanks
and put it back to the narrow trail again. He knew none of
this land, knew only the direction in which Tracy
Cawdrey's spread lay, but he felt no inward concern. All
his life he had grown used to land such as this, a vast
stretching territory of lakes and mountains, parched alkali
flats and broad rivers. The pattern was always basically the
same, no matter where one went, and he always managed
to feel at home with the bright stars over his head for a
blanket and the quiet earth under his feet.

By degrees the country roughened as he continued to
follow an upwards trail. The horse's shoes struck fire from
the rocks as it clambered over then and here and there,
huge, upthrusting pinnacles loomed over him, thrusting

themselves a hundred feet or so into the air about him.
Going down the other side of the hills he kept in the shelter of a long stretch of pines. Here there were vague
murmurings that he tried to place. The faint gurgle of a
stream that flowed with a bubbling swiftly down a rocky
slope. The undulating, weird howl of a coyote in the
desert somewhere, the sound carrying well in the clear,
cold air.

Clouds came up, hiding the moon before it had a
chance to set and rain dripped steadily from them, striking the brim of his hat, soaking into his shirt. It was a cool,
continuous rain that grew heavier as the minutes passed
and the clouds gathered more thickly overhead. Clem
shivered in the saddle, lowered his head even further and
kept the horse moving with an even gait.

Passing through the low foothills he came out on to the
wide plain that stretched for the best part of thirty miles
until it reached clear to the other side of the Cawdrey
spread.

In place of the hard rock and dirt there was now thick,
lush grass and soft earth under it. Here he made good
time, as he had expected, keeping his eyes and ears alert
for trouble. It wasn't likely that he would bump into any of
the Texas Dusters here on Cawdrey's land so close to the
ranch, but there seemed little doubt that as they grew
stronger in numbers they also grew more audacious.

The land was, however, deceptive. The grasslands
seemed to stretch on for mile upon mile and there was a
greying in the eastern part of the sky by the time he
topped a low rise and found himself looking down on the
ranch-house. He rode slowly down into the courtyard,
noticed that there were several horses in the corral. He
opened the wooden gate, slapped his own mount inside
after unsaddling, stood for a moment with the still-cool
breeze of early morning blowing into his face, then turned

and walked over the hard-packed dirt of the courtyard towards the house. A light had snapped on in one of the windows as he approached, the door opened and two men stood there, one holding a Winchester.

'Who's out there?' Cawdrey's voice, harsh and authoritative.

'Clem Winters,' he called back and strode forward, keeping his hands well away from his guns. With the rustlers about there was the distinct possibility that men would be more trigger happy than normal around these parts and he didn't fancy a rifle bullet in him by mistake.

The other still held the barrel of the Winchester high, but as Clem came out into the light he lowered it. 'You seem to have ridden out here in a hurry, is there something wrong?'

'Plenty, but we may be able to turn it to our advantage. That's why I had to come out to see you right away.'

'Come inside, Winters.' The other stood on one side to let him pass, then closed the door. 'I'll get some hot coffee made for us.'

Five minutes later, as they sat in the parlour of the ranch-house, Clem, leaning back in his chair, relaxing, realizing only then how taut he had been during the whole of that ride across country, told the other what had happened in Bitter Ridge.

Cawdrey listened intently and in silence until he had finished, and then got to his feet, slapping his bunched fist into the palm of his other hand.

'If you're sure that false message of yours got through to the raiders, then we've got the chance to finish them for good. I can get as many of my men together as I can spare and when they attack the west herd we'll kill them all.' He closed his teeth with an audible snap. 'This is what we've been waiting for. A chance to meet up with them face to face and fight it out on fair and equal terms. So far they've

116

always succeeded in drifting away into the hills before we could catch up with them. This time they might not be so lucky.'

'What concerns me more than anything else,' said Clem slowly, sipping his coffee, 'is how Haswell managed to get through to these men. That line goes clear to Twin Buttes and then beyond. Even if the telegraph operator in Twin Buttes is in league with them as well, how does he get word through to them, if it's true what the sheriff says, that they've had no trouble at all with these rustlers.'

'That isn't too difficult to explain,' maintained the other. He turned from the window, his face serious. 'All they have to do is tap the line anywhere out there where it crossed the hills. They probably send their messages at a certain time every night and have a man listening out for any calls.'

Clem nodded. It made sense. There was sure to be someone among them who knew a little about the telegraph and how it worked.

'By the way, I reckon you ought to know that somebody shot Doc on his way back to town. Plugged him in the arm. He ought to be back on his feet in a couple of days according to Doc Barcroft, but he won't be using a gun for a little while.'

Cawdrey tightened his lips at the news. 'That's bad. Any idea who it was?'

'Too dark. He didn't recognize any of them, but he reckons he got one.'

'If our plan works, we'll get the whole bunch,' muttered the other fiercely. 'Then maybe this territory will be a safe place in which to live. So far, those hills have been the refuge of any hellbender running from the law and nobody has been able to flush them out. It's small wonder they've managed to plague us for so long.'

'You got any men who can follow a trail in your outfit?'

'Sure, Indian Mike is one of the best there is. You figure on needing him?'

'We may. If any of them decide to make a break for it they may lead us back into the hills to their hideout. I'd like to be able to follow their trail.'

Cawdrey got to his feet, picked up the long-barrelled Winchester from where it stood against the wall. 'I'll get the men together,' he said tightly. 'They may attack the herd tonight and I want all of the men I can spare out there and in position. We can't afford to have anything go wrong this time.'

Clem heard the sound of distant horses moving out of the grey dawn a few moments before he spotted them, a bunch of men riding down the nearer slope of one of the hills. They rode into the wide courtyard and slid from the saddle, their mounts moving in the direction of the water troughs. Clem recognized a handful of them as men who had been with Tracy Cawdrey when he had first met up with the rancher. One was the man who had been plugged in the shoulder by the raider. He had his arm strapped up but he still managed to ride his mount and it was obvious he intended to ride with them.

Cawdrey came out of the house, stood for a moment in the grey light of dawn looking about him. There was an odd tightness to his lined face which Cleni could not recall having seen before. Then he walked into the yard to where his horse stood near the gate of the corral, already saddled. Thrusting the Winchester into the leather scabbard by the saddle, he swung himself up with a deceptive ease, sat tall and straight, his eyes flicking over the men who had now mounted and sat at the back of him, ready to move out when he gave the word.

For an instant he sat silent, then his gaze switched to Clem. 'You set this up for us,' he said, and his voice sounded strangely distant. 'I reckon we owe it to you to let you ride with us.'

Clem had already swung his horse into line as if that had been a foregone conclusion. He nodded slightly, Cawdrey stared hard at him for a moment, then turned and waved the men forward, out of the courtyard and on to the trail that wound north-west of the ranch. The tall grass that grew on the edge of the trail was still wet with the night's rain, but the sun would soon be up, steaming the moisture off it as the heat head rose.

By mid-morning the heat was a burning pressure on their backs. The country around them, in every direction, blazed with it, the ground shivered whenever men lifted their heads to peer into the distance and the skyline was never still but shimmered as if water were flowing in front of it. They left the wide range, moved out into the dry, burnt-brown grass and rocks that separated the home spread from the grassland which lay to the northwest, nestling against the base of the tall hills. Somewhere in those hills, thought Clem tightly, were the raiders they meant to smash and among them a killer named Goudie.

He clenched his teeth more tightly together as he remembered how these men had jumped Doc the previous night. He had been lucky to get away with his life. Whether the killers had recognized him or whether they just figured he was another of Cawdrey's men riding back from the ranch, he did not know. But he was certain in his own mind who those men had been. Maybe Goudie had been one of those three men.

The thought was a living flame in his brain. He tried to control it, knowing that when the showdown came he would need all the coolness in his mind there was. An angry man could be quick on the draw, but he was more inclined to waste shots than one with an ice-cool brain.

At noon they camped among the rocks where a narrow

stream came rushing down from the hills, clear-crystal water that still held the coolness of the tall summits in it. Clem lay belly-flat with the others and drank on the upstream side of the horses, letting his mount drift to graze in the coarse grass that grew along either bank of the stream. Building a smoke, he sat down with the others, hat pulled well down over his eyes in the harsh sunglare.

Cawdrey came over and lowered himself stiffly to the hard ground beside him.

Clem said, eyeing the men scattered around, 'You figure you have enough men here to take on that hunch if they show up in the right place?'

'I reckon so,' he grinned. 'There's no need to bother yourself. We've got enough here to handle that wild bunch. All we want is the chance to meet them face to face before they can fade right back into those hills.'

Clem nodded. He caught a glimpse of the grizzled old man who had ridden with them, squatting with a bunch of men on the far side of the stream. Cawdrey followed his glance. 'That's Indian Mike,' he said slowly. 'I reckon he can trail a bobcat through the mountains. Never seen him stuck yet, unless the rain had washed the trail away completely. Even then he could pick out signs that any other man would have missed completely.'

'We may need him if they do decide to break for it. There's always the chance that somebody back in town has managed to get through to 'em and warn 'em that Haswell is dead. It may make them change their plans a little, especially if they figure out that the message could have been a trick.'

'What's the chance of that happening?' There was a momentary look of concern on the older man's features.

'Difficult to say. I know that Haswell had friends in town. There were some in the saloon who must've seen me talking with him. Reckon they might figure that I shot him down to prevent him from warning the wild bunch that this was a trap.'

'We'll soon know. If they have been warned, then they won't show up tonight.'

'They may attack the other herd.'

'That's a risk I've got to take. I'll chance that if there's the slightest chance of getting them out into the open.'

The sun held at its zenith as they ate, then saddled up and continued to ride, keeping the sun behind them now, throwing short shadows in front of their mounts. They rode over the hot rock floor of a deep bowl in the hills. Once a river had made its way down here, cutting a channel through the solid rock, smoothing it over long ages. Now the river had been dried up for centuries and only the smooth bed remained, showing where the water had travelled. The rocky walls on either side of them rose sheer for fifty or a hundred feet, only occasionally did they fall away leaving small islands of red sandstone bordering the trail.

Cawdrey seemed to know his way intimately. Once he paused on a spur of rock and stared out in front of him. They had been climbing ever since they had left the stream and riding forward until he was just behind the other. Clem was surprised to find how high they were above the valley that lay spread out below them. From their vantage point they could see for miles in every direction. Stretching away in front of them, the plain ran out to the horizon, where it blended with the purple haze that seemed to spread itself around the entire rim of the world. The sunlight threw stark shadows over everything, and seemed to have burned the colour out of the rocks and vegetation so that there were only drab hues below them. Even the welcome green of the lush grass seemed to be missing.

Cawdrey pointed off to his right. 'The raiders must have

their hide-out somewhere off in those hills yonder. We tracked them into the foothills on one occasion, then lost the trail. The whole area is honeycombed with mine workings and it's my belief that they're hiding out inside the hill, in one of those tunnels.'

'Why don't you try hunting for them in there?'

'Wouldn't do any good. Those tunnels are nearly all linked up with each other inside. We would have to know exactly where they were or we'd never find them. Not only that, but they know this territory far better than we do, and we could lose most of our force if we attempted to go in there after them without some kind of plan.'

'Sounds reasonable,' nodded Clem. He ran his gaze over the blue-hazed hills in the distance, perhaps ten miles away. They seemed quiet as they slumbered in the sunlight, but it was a brooding quiet that lay uneasy and heavy over them.

'Nothing along the trails down there.' Cawdrey jerked a thumb in the direction of the narrow trails they could just make out far below them. To their left, running diagonally across their line of view, was the broad ribbon of the stage road that winds its way around the northern edge of the desertlands until it reached Twin Buttes.

'It ain't likely that those critters will be out in broad daylight,' said one of the men harshly.

'They may figure that they're safe enough in these hills,' Clem said pointedly. 'Besides, if they think this may be a trap, they may be scouting the hills on the lookout for any party moving along the trail through the rocks.'

Clem saw the other's eyes show uncertainty at that. He drew in a sharp breath and lost some of his cheerfulness.

By mid-afternoon they were riding the downgrade. Here the country was more open and Clem had the uneasy feeling that they were being watched all the way. The feeling had been with him since they had left the summit of the trail and moved out of the rocks. It had grown over the minutes and hours, something that he could sense, but could not put his finger on. He tried to slit his gaze against the all-consuming glare, to spot anything that moved, the glint of sunlight shining off a rifle barrel or the movement of riders in the distance, crowding in on them. He thought about it as he rode and was troubled.

Again the terrain changed. The rocks were left behind, they dipped down into the grasslands once more, rode through wire that had been laid around the perimeter of the pasture. Ahead of them, in the hazy distance, Clem caught a glimpse of the herd, could make out the lowing of the cattle on the still, dust-filled air.

'Three thousand head there,' said Cawdrey soberly. 'It's a mighty big temptation to those cattle thieves.'

'Let's hope they swallow the bait and come,' murmured Clem. He rode beside the other, looking about him with interest. In the distance he could make out the shapes of the riders, moving around the herd, counted five of them on the far side.

'You figure it may be tonight?' Cawdrey turned his head, sunlight glinting off the silver hair.

'For our sakes, I hope so. The men are going to become ornery if they have to hang around here for any length of time for a bunch of raiders that never shows up.'

Clem shoved the broad-brimmed hat well back on to his head and squinted up at the sun as it began its western lowering over the sky. Now that it was moving away from the zenith, a little of the colour was coming back into the terrain around them. They picked their way slowly towards the herd. The trail here was not well marked. Soon, however, they entered sheltering trees and the air held a green coolness that had been missing all the way along the trail.

'We'll eat and then take up our positions,' Cawdrey said tightly. Now that the moment of showdown was approaching fast, he seemed tightly keyed up. Every move he made was quick and jerky and Clem could guess at the emotion which was riding the rancher hard. For several years they had been plagued by this bunch of rustlers moving down out of the hills at night, without warning, striking almost where they pleased, taking off the beef and driving it out into the desert and then up towards the empty hills where they were able to keep the beef until driving it clear out of the territory.

Darkness fell slowly in this country. They could see the twilight move out of the east while there was still a vivid splash of red in the west, covering the place where the sun had dropped out of sight behind the mountains that grew up on the horizon, spiking the still-bright sky. Slowly, however, the reds and yellows were giving way to the deeper hues, the cooler blues and greens.

'Where do you reckon they'll try to hit the herd?' Clem looked about him as he spoke. He had eaten the hastily prepared meal and the weariness of the long ride had given way to a feeling of well being.

'Down from the hills in that direction, I reckon.' The rancher gave a quick nod towards the east. 'There's an old Indian trail leading down from the hills there and if they want to come down quiet, that's the way to do it.'

Clem narrowed his gaze. Shadows were falling thick and huge over the country now but he could just make out the switchback course of the narrow trail where it stood out in the twilight, etched out against the darker hue of the hills. Sparse vegetation still clung to the rocks there, he noticed, and there were clumps of stunted trees and thorn which could provide plenty of shelter to the raiders as they approached.

Ten minutes later all of the colour had been wiped

from the western sky and the darkness came in, pushing away all sign of daylight. Leaving only the five men to guard the herd, the others mounted up and made their way over the plain towards the low hills, well to one side of the Indian trail where it came down from the rocky hills on to the grasslands. Here the land proved to be deceptive. The bushes provided them with plenty of cover and it was possible to tether their horses with slip ropes, ready to jerk them free at a moment's notice and ride out in pursuit of the raiders if they turned and tried to make a break for it once the guns opened up and they realized they had been outsmarted, and lured into a trap.

Crouching down in a small hollow, Clem glanced about him at the rest of the men. Grim-faced, eyes narrowed a little, they stood around in a loose group, eyes alert, watching the hills that lay above them, looming up into the dark heavens now that they were so close to them.

His throat felt dry, but he knew that it would be fatal to roll himself a smoke. The red tip of a cigarette, or the brief flare of a sulphur match could be seen for miles in that country and if they gave themselves away to the rustlers it could mean they would scare off the wild bunch for good and their chance of catching them in the open would be gone.

Slowly the tension began to mount. The men talked in low whispers or stood around in silence. Nobody fooled themselves that it was going to be easy even if the raiders did show up on time and could be taken by surprise. There was undoubtedly no better way of smashing them than this and if the plan failed, if for some reason the rustlers did not come, or had guessed that this might be a trick, it might be impossible to stop them at all. Clem found himself thinking of Goudie again and the tightness came back into his body. With an effort he forced himself to relax.

The quietness of the hills lay around them, pressing in on them from all sides. Overhead the sky was clear with a pale moon hanging low in the west, throwing a yellow glow over the mountains on the distant skyline. It would not provide them with too much light, thought Clem inwardly, and by midnight it would probably have set and they would have to work in almost complete darkness.

A man nearby groaned and straightened from his cramped position, and muttered a harsh curse under his breath. 'It doesn't look as though they're coming tonight,' he grunted.

If they do come, we're ready for 'em.' Clem pushed himself forward until he was lying against the cold rock, eyes pushing ahead into the darkness that lay thickly around them. If the raiders were coming, they would be on their way by now, he thought, heading down through the hills from their hideout. They would not have much time. Everything would depend on them driving off any guards there might be and getting the cattle up into the hills and out of sight before dawn, or before the sound of gunfire could bring anyone running to the scene.

A voice came clearly to him from among the men. 'I heard something there, up in the hills. Sounded like horses headed this way.'

'You sure of that?' Clem spoke quickly in a hushed tone.

A shadow detached itself from the others and came in his direction. He recognized the foreman of the ranch. The man nodded, pointed. 'Up there,' he said decisively. 'Along the trail. Still a fewmiles away, I reckon.'

Clem strained his ears to pick out the faintest sound in the distance. For a long moment he stood there, head cocked a little to one side. Then he shook his head slowly. 'I don't hear anything.'

'I'm damned sure I did,' declared the other emphatically.

A minute passed and then, high above them, just on the limit of hearing, he picked out the dull muted sound of riders.

'Here they come,' Cawdrey's voice came out of the darkness. 'Everybody ready? I don't want any mistakes now. This may be the only chance we've got of smashing this goddarned bunch. I don't want anybody to fire or give away his position until I give the signal. Understand?'

There were low murmurs of assent from the men as they crouched down among the rocks. Out of the corner of his eye, Clem saw the dark mass of the herd as it milled around, bedding down for the night. He could just make out the mournful cries of the herders as they rode guard around its rim, keeping them moving for a period until they had settled down. It was just possible that the herd might detect the horses moving in on them from the trail and if they were spooked in that way, it could add to their difficulties.

He finally turned back and slid the gun from its holster, balancing it in the palm of his hand. From where he stood he noticed that the herd looked quite innocent out there and there was no indication of the gunmen lying in wait among the rocks.

The thunder of the advancing riders grew in their ears. They seemed to be riding straight in along the trail, not attempting to hide the fact that they were there. He grinned tightly to himself in the darkness. They must be feeling really confident, sure of themselves, to come into the attack like that. It seemed reasonable to believe that the message that Haswell had sent out to them over the telegraph had been received and was being acted on.

Cawdrey came up beside him, stood in the darkness, staring out towards the hills. 'Whatever happens, this time we don't want to give them the chance to spook that herd and start them stampeding. If they do that, they might manage to get away before we can get on their trail.'

'Do the herders know what to do when they move down into the plain?'

Cawdrey nodded. It was impossible to make out the expression on his face as he looked out into the darkness. 'They'll carry out their orders. Five of my best men.' From the rocks some distance ahead, the hoofbeats of approaching horses sounded crisply now in the clear, cold air of night They were perhaps half a mile away, moving out of the shelter of the stunted trees. Clem checked his gun, glanced back instinctively to where the horses had been tethered among the rocks.

'There they are,' Cawdrey's hoarse whisper was a tight sound close by. Clem jerked his head round, narrowed his eyes and almost at once picked out the tightpacked bunch of horsemen who moved out of the low hills and paused for a moment on the edge of the plain. A moment fled before he realized what they were doing, then he saw they were pushing up their neck pieces to cover their faces, ready to ride in. With an effort he forced the grim tightness from his body, sucked in a deep breath and held it in his lungs for a long moment. Around him he heard the slow movements of the men as they waited for Cawdrey's signal. They had to allow the raiders a chance to ride out on to the plains and move well away from the trail leading back into the hills. Once they managed to do that they would be able to swing across and cut off their way of escape.

'Get to your horses.' Cawdrey gave the order sharply.

Swiftly the men scattered, ran for their mounts, swung up into the saddle. Clem stepped into the saddle and sat easily. All of the weariness had gone from his body now and it was as if every sense had become sharpened by the mere sight of those men sitting their horses less than half a mile away.

'Let them get into the plains,' Cawdrey called.

Ahead of their position the night came alive with thudding hoofs as the rustlers headed towards the herd, yelling and shouting at the tops of their voices. Gunshots rang out and Clem could just make out the stabbing muzzle flashes in the darkness as the men rode down on the herd.

'Get moving,' Cawdrey yelled the words at the top of his voice. Even as he did so, he spurred his own mount out of cover from the rocks and urged it in the direction of the racing bunch of riders. Clem rode low in the saddle, gun out, heels flailing against the horse's ribs as he urged it forward. A gun roared in the night from close beside him as one of the men opened fire. The raider pack were still swinging in towards the herd, still unaware of their presence there, so intent on what they had in hand, that they failed to notice the men who rode vengefully at their backs.

A torch flared suddenly and then another as the rustlers moved in on the far side of the herd. Clem changed course. He was now between the rustlers and the trail to the north, and there were several of Cawdrey's men with him. Swinging, they blasted off more shots and one of the raiders suddenly threw up his arms and toppled sideways from the saddle. His mount dragged him for several yards as his booted foot caught in the stirrups. Then his legs were jerked free as the horse plunged on and he lay still while the riderless horse cantered away from the others.

One of the men carrying a flaming torch was also hit. He wobbled in the saddle, managed to hold on to the torch for a second, then released his hold on it and it dropped into the grass. Fortunately the rain of the previous night had damped the ground sufficiently to prevent the grass going on fire and the light of the fallen torch went out a moment later.

By now the raiders were aware of the danger which threatened them from their rear. Clem saw them pulling round on their reins, striving to turn their horses and head them back from the herd. They had clearly realized that it would not be possible to stampede the herd and they were merely intent on making their escape from the traps into which they had fallen.

'Don't let them make it back into the hills,' called Cawdrey. 'Ride them down. Every last one of them.'

Two men crowded Clem to the right and he swung his mount heavily against them. They backed off, continued to race their mounts forward after the raiders, who were swinging wide now, in an attempt to work their way around the Cawdrey men in the darkness.

'Spread out more,' he heard Cawdrey shout. There was a grim desperation in his voice. Another man bellowed something to the right, swung up his arm to point. A second later a shot took him in the chest and he toppled out of the saddle and crashed to the ground, where he lay still, a heap of unmoving shadow in the thick grass.

Five of the rustlers had been hit, but the remainder of the bunch, swinging round in a wide arc, were racing back towards the hills, firing as they went. Clem spurred his mount after them. A slug took a piece out of the saddle an inch from his body. Another hummed viciously over his head and lost itself in the distance.

There was a singing tension in Clem's body, sweeping along every muscle and fibre, and there was a grim, vicious excitement in his brain. He touched spurs to his mount, felt the animal respond magnificently even though it had been on the trail all day, leaping forward through the soft grass. Ahead of him the hills loomed up against the starlit sky. Crowding in, the men of the Cawdrey bunch came racing over the plains, firing savagely as they tried to head off the main bunch of rustlers.

With a sinking sensation, Clem realized that they weren't going to make it. Two more of the raiders pitched from their saddles, but the others raced on, their horses evidently fresher and faster than those of their pursuers. Out of the corner of his eye, Clem made out Cawdrey's tall figure, waving the men forward urgently. Already, the other was visualizing the rustlers getting away scot-free.

The shouting and firing went on. Men rode in from the flanks and fired at the raiders as they tried to slip through into the hills. They were about evenly matched, it was true, but the rustlers were in no mood to stay and fight it out with these gunfighters. They would only fight if the odds were overwhelmingly in their favour. When things were as even as this they had no heart for fighting. They preferred to strike out of the darkness of the hills, to strike suddenly and without warning, against little or no opposition.

Jostling, thrusting, the raiders rode along the narrow trail and began to pull away up into the hills. Clem heard their hoofbeats as they struck the solid rock. He emptied his gun after them, heard one man cry out loudly, but it was impossible to see whether he had been killed or merely wounded. All of the raiders were struggling to get away along that narrow trail, slugging and cursing one another as they were all jammed together.

Then, out of the babble of voices, he picked out one that he recognized instantly, one that stood out in his memory and sent a little shiver coursing along his body. Goudie's voice. There was no mistaking it. He had heard it several times in the past when he had almost caught up with the killer. Now he picked it out again, thin and high-pitched, almost like a woman's. rising through several octaves as the man yelled something furiously. But it was impossible from the mere sound of the voice to pick out the man himself in that crowded bunch of shadowy figures as they struggled up into the rocks. Already, half of them were out of sight around a sharp bend in the trail, although he could still hear the sound of hoofbeats hammering on the rocky surface of the track.

'Get in after 'em!' shouted Cawdrey harshly. He came riding forward, then pulled up sharply as a burst of fire came hammering out of the rocks.

'Get down,' Cleni yelled urgently. 'They've left a couple of men behind to hold us off. They're up there in the rocks to the right.' A bullet tore through the air close to his head and he flung himself from the saddle, running for the rocks.

There was no doubt in his mind what had to be done now. He could hear Cawdrey shouting to him to get back into the saddle, that they would ride those two killers down. That, he knew would be not only dangerous, but foolish. Up thère, two men would be able to hold them off until Kingdom Come. It was only possible for two men at most to ride abreast along the trail at that point, and it would be the easiest thing in the world for those two men to shoot down two riders before they had a chance even to draw level with their position. It would take them even longer to spot the concealed man in the dark.

Hurling himself forward, with a harsh, shrill whistle of a ricochet whining in his ears, he hit the rock with a blow that almost knocked the wind completely from his lungs. He heard the men behind him send a volley of withering fire into the rocks, but knew that it would be almost impossible for them to hit either of the two men crouched down there.

'Hold your fire,' called Cawdrey. He must have realized that Clem's plan was the only one that offered any chance of success, even though it meant they would be held up for several precious minutes.

Heaving himself forward, Clem moved among the boulders and loose rocks, striving to keep a foothold there without giving his position away to the waiting men. At any moment he expected to hear the sharp bark of a revolver and feel the smashing impact of lead striking his body. If only there had been enough light for him to see by, he thought grimly. Then he pushed the thought away as he realized that this would work two ways and it would be easier for the rustlers to pick him out in the moonlight.

There was the sound of a boot scraping on rock just a few feet above him. He paused and pressed his body tightly into the hard rock, felt an out-thrusting corner of rock press tightly and painfully into his groin. Pulling back his head he tried to make out the other's position. There was a large boulder immediately over his head and he guessed that was the logical place for them to have concealed themselves, a place where they could keep a close watch on the trail below without having to expose themselves to the murderous fire which could be poured into them.

A couple of sharp cracks as they loosed off two more shots in the direction of the men down on the plain, their mounts milling around restlessly as their riders strove to hold them in check.

For a long moment there was silence. Then he clearly picked out the sharp gust of sound as one of the men let his breath go. His nervousness had given him away. Evidently unable to bear the suspense and knowing that someone had slid from the saddle and was working his way towards them, the other had been holding his breath while he had tried to pick out any sign of danger.

Every muscle in Clem's body was so tight that it began to ache intolerably and he levered himself forward a couple of feet, working around the boulder. Coming out a little above it, he saw the two dark shapes crouched there, peering down through a gap in the rocks. There was no time to waste. Already the sound of the bulk of the riders was fading swiftly in the distance as they hurried to make their getaway. Stepping forward, he levelled the Colt on the two men and said harshly:

'All right. Step away from there real easy and—'

Swiftly, both men whirled at the sound, bringing up their guns to level them on Clem's body. But it was a move he had expected. They were still turning when the gun in his right hand blasted twice. The taller of the two crashed back against the rock, the gun dropping from his nerveless fingers to clatter on to the rocks, arms spread wide in a death-act of crucifixion. The other jerked as the bullet took him in the chest. He fell forward, the gun in his hand going off with a loud sound. The bullet struck the rock a couple of feet in front of him and ricocheted into the distance with the high-pitched wail of tortured metal.

His mind was very clear now, very sharp. He heard every sound below with a curiously magnified importance. Going out on to the trail he moved downward, his feet slipping on the loose rocks underfoot.

'Everything all right up there, Winters?' roared Cawdrey at the top of his voice. He gigged his mount forward on to the upgrade trail without waiting for any reply.

'They're both dead,' Clem called, reached his own mount and swung up into the saddle, following the bunch of men as they rode into the hills behind Cawdrey. There was something driving the old rancher now, thought Clem tightly. Maybe it was the continued loss of his cattle over the years; or perhaps it was something more, something that went deeper than that. There was some kind of mystery about the silver-haired rancher. Clem had felt it from the first moment he had met up with the other. It was as if there was a deep and rising hatred driving him on.

They circled swiftly up the narrow, winding Indian trail, until they were high in the hills. Ahead of them it was still possible to pick out the sound of the fleeing bunch of men and Clem guessed that as long as they were able to hear that they would have little difficulty in following them.

Even in the darkness there was light enough from the thin slice of the moon and the bright stars, for them to see most of the details of their surroundings. The country here was rugged, fit only for the prospectors who had moved up into it in the years past, working the seams and the narrow, swift-rushing streams for gold. There had been some discovered there, but not enough for many seams to have been opened up, although, as Cawdrey had pointed out earlier, several of the main seams had been sufficiently rich for them to have been tunnelled into the hillside further into the hills, the power of explosives having superseded the pick and shovel of the smaller prospector.

They crossed a boulder-strewn plateau, here sufficiently broad for most of them to ride side by side. The tall rocks crowded on the edge of the flat stretch of rock and for a moment as they rode swiftly across it in the cold darkness, with the wind blowing in their faces, Clem had the impression that this could be a trap laid especially for them. If those men had stopped and were lying in wait for them among the rocks that looked down on this flat plateau, it would be a massacre if they opened up with all of the fire-power they had.

But they crossed the plateau in safety without a shot being fired from the darkness and on the far side Cawdrey called a halt, reining his mount so sharply and unexpectedly that it reared, forelegs striking at the air, teetering on the edge of the rocks.

The men halted and sat their mounts, listening. There was no sound except for the heavy gale of the horses' breathing. Cawdrey turned his head in every direction, lips pressed into a tight line in the shadow of his face.

'They've gone to ground.' His voice rasped harshly

135

across the stillness. He looked around him at the men gathered around. 'Where's Indian Mike?'

The old man pushed his way out of the crowd. 'Here boss.'

'We know they came this way. Reckon you can pick up their trail from here? They must have cut through the pass yonder.' Cawdrey pointed. There was one solitary opening in the rocks that lay jumbled ahead of them in a mass of ragged shadow.

Indian Mike moved his mount forward at a walking pace. There was not the same need to hurry now. Without the sound of their horses to follow, they were like blind men groping in the dark, relying on one man to pick up the trail.

Clem sat tight in his saddle, watching as the old man moved along the trail. He had heard of men such as this, men who had run with the Indians during the old days, who had learned the secrets of following a trail when ordinary men could see nothing.

'Here's where they headed, boss.' Indian Mike called softly out of the darkness at the end of the narrow trail where it passed between the rising columns of rock.

Cawdrey rode up with Clem close behind him. Indian Mike pointed. At first, Clem could see nothing, then he noticed where a horse had kicked rock from an outjutting ledge. There was also a dark stain there. Indian Mike pointed towards it.

'Blood,' he said simply. 'One of them at least has been hurt – and bad.'

Cawdrey lifted his head and stared along the trail. About a mile further along the tall butments of sandstone lifted high. If they were in there, thought Clem tightly, they might never find them.

136

CHAPTER SEVEN

FINAL
SHOWDOWN

Everything was ominously quiet as they edged their mounts closer to the rising wall of rock which loomed high in front of them. Here, Clem saw, the trail ended. Perhaps, in the past it had continued on through the hills and over the top to the desert which lay to the east. But it could easily have been obliterated when they had been blasting for gold among the hills. In the dimness, as they reined their mounts in the shadows, he could see the dull metal of rusted rail that went down into the deep bowels of the earth. The open mouths of the tunnels showed dark, like empty eyes, watching them ominously.

Clem could feel the tension mounting in the men now. They did not doubt that they had reached the end of the trail, that the hideout of the rustlers was here, in one of those dark tunnels, that there might even be a tunnel that led all the way through the hills, out towards the edge of the desert, and it might be along this that the raiders drove their herds once they had run them off the range.

Clem steadied himself in the saddle, feeling the silence

grow, holding his body tautly upright, ready for the slight-est sound of danger. He did not think that the rustlers had gone very far into the hills. They were not such fools as to leave the entrance to their hideout unguarded, especially as they must have been fairly sure they were following close on their tails.

The men began to edge their mounts sideways at a signal from Cawdrey, spreading out in a wide arc to face the old mine workings. Tracy Cawdrey edged his mount forward until he was beside Clem. He said in a hoarse whisper: 'I've seen many a trap in my lifetime and this one has the same kind of smell about it.'

'I agree,' Clem gave a tight nod. 'They're in there some-where and just waiting for us to go forward into killing range. I've got the feel of eyes boring into me already.' He eased the sixers in their holsters. Here, they were less than a couple of hundred yards from the nearest tunnel in the bare rock. To go forward on horseback would be to court disaster.

Clem sensed the men staring at Cawdrey and himself in the cold darkness, waiting for a signal to go in to the attack. But Cawdrey was clearly in no hurry to give such a signal.

'You reckon it might be wise to watch our step?' He turned to Clem, clearly believing that the other's advice here would be valuable.

Clem nodded. If we rush in there, we're running the risk of being shot to pieces before we get within range of them. Remember that they can see us moving across the open space, while we can't see them in there. Very likely they expect we'll try to rush 'em. Trouble is, that we don't know which of those tunnels they're in.'

'What do you suggest we do?'

'I reckon there's only one thing, one or two men to make their way forward without being seen. At worst, if they're discovered, they'll draw their fire and that should give the others a good chance.'

'I'll get a couple of men . . .' began the other, then paused as Clem stopped him with an outstretched hand.

'I'll go. I've had experience with critters like these. Besides, there's a man in there I want. He's still alive and still with 'em.'

Cawdrey shrugged. 'Go ahead. We'll cover you if anything starts.'

Clem slid from the saddle, checked the twin Colts. Very slowly he eased his way forward, aware of the men at his back taking up their positions around the mine workings. In the vast open area that faced the tall, sheer side of the hill, there was not a single drop of cover, no bushes, no vegetation of any kind. Nothing to give shelter from gunfire aimed at him from the tunnels.

Swiftly he surveyed the area where the faint, pale moonlight fell on it, throwing too many shadows for his liking. There were a hundred places where gunmen could hide, ready to throw lead at him without warning and the knowledge that the other men were at his back, ready to return the fire and afford him some degree of cover, gave him little comfort.

More than ever before the feeling was strong within him that men had been posted somewhere at the entrance to the tunnels, ready to open fire on anyone who tried to work forward, but that was a risk he would have to take. Slithering forward on hands and knees, taking care not to let the guns strike against the rocks, he wormed his way forward until he had reached a point less than fifty feet from the bare rock face. Still no shot had been fired at him which indicated that he had either reached that point unseen and unheard, or they were waiting for him to get closer before dropping him.

He paused, held his breath, tried to pick out any sound

that might give him an indication of where the enemy might be. But there was a deep stillness lying over everything and not even the snicker of a horse broke that silence. He felt a little quiver pass through his body, forced himself to go on, eyes alert, swinging slowly from one side to the other, looking for any movement, ready to swing to meet it when it came.

Scuttling to one side, he came up against a rocky escarpment that ran around the rim of the plateau. From there he could work his way around to the old workings, keeping into the shadows. This was the only way to reach them that gave him any chance at all of doing it unseen. Slowly he eased himself upright, pressed his body into the sharply-angled corners of rock that cut painfully into his flesh as he scraped past them, scarcely daring to breathe. Once a rock moved under his questing fingers, threatened to roll down the sheer face and bounce out across the open ground. Swiftly, instinctively, his fingers curled around it, caught it before it fell.

Five minutes later, with the feeling that this was more of a trap than ever, he reached the old tumble-down hut that stood close to the nearest tunnel. Cautiously, he worked his way towards it, made sure that the place was deserted, and then moved over to the mouth of the tunnel. In the dimness, he could make out the long, thick wooden beams which criss-crossed under the low roof of rock and the rails which he had noticed outside, ran deep into the tunnel, vanishing into the darkness. There were a couple of rusted wagons which had evidently been used to transport the ore back to the surface lying close by and he crouched down behind them, staring out into the pitch blackness which yawned in front of him. There was no sound in that long, stretching tunnel and the smooth dust underfoot seemed to have lain undisturbed for long years.

Clearly the rustlers had not come in here. Quite possibly it was a dead end, only went so far into the solid rock and then stopped. They would not use a tunnel which could turn out to be a trap. The one they would use would have a second exit somewhere, coming out among the rocks that lay in the distance.

Small wonder, he thought tightly, that they had never been caught, if this was the case.

Gently, he eased the sixers from their holsters, the faint whisper of sound as they cleared leather lost in the darkness. Treading carefully, he went forward to the entrance of the tunnel, moved out into the open – and into danger! The savage burst of gunfire from the darkness to his left sent lead hurtling through the air close to his head, slugs slashing off the rocks, screeching into the darkness. The thunder of more gunfire ripped across the cool night air as the men crouched down among the rocks with Cawdrey opened fire to give him cover. He ducked back into the tunnel as shots whistled dangerously close from both sides. It would be an ironical thing if he was shot down by a bullet fired by one of the men he was trying to help.

He fired three swift shots into the darkness, thought he heard a man cry out as one of the slugs found its mark. Then there was more pandemonium as gunfire rattled and echoed from one rocky wall to the other. Muzzles flashed and gave away the gunmen on both sides. A rifle barked savagely, the sound booming above the sharper note of the Colts. Something scorched along Clem's shoulder ripping away part of his shirt. leaving a thin smear of blood on his shirt.

He drew back sharply under cover, cursing himself for having exposed himself to that accurate fire. Crouched there in the pitch blackness of the other tunnels, it would be relatively simple for the rustlers to spot him, to notice every movement he made, whereas he could not see any of them clearly and they would be wary enough to change their positions after firing off a couple of shots.

A harsh voice yelled suddenly, over the gunfire. 'Better get on your horses and ride back out of here, Cawdrey. If you don't, we'll shoot down all of you.'

Cawdrey's reply came instantly. 'Why don't you give up, all of you. You don't stand a chance now that you've been cornered. If you don't throw out your guns and come out into the open with your hands lifted high where we can see 'ern, we'll come in and get you.'

A harsh laugh sounded. 'We figured that sooner or later you might be lucky and follow us this far. Could be you reckon we're caught in a trap. The trouble is it's you who're in a trap. You've ridden right into big trouble.'

'You can't fool us.' There was a tight note of anger in Cawdrey's tone. 'I've sworn I'd hunt you down, Warburg. Now I've got you cornered, I don't intend to leave until you're all dead.'

'So you know that I'm the leader of this band, Cawdrey? I wondered how long it would take you to realize that.'

'I've known for some time.' The firing had ceased now, as all attention seemed to be focused on the two men. While listening with half an ear, Clem took the opportunity to slither forward on his belly, keeping his head and shoulders down, edging towards the small hut which stood a dozen yards away, to one side of the wide tunnel in which the rustlers were holed up.

'You don't seem to have been able to do much about it. I've run your cattle off the range, stopped any of your hired gunmen who tried to prevent me. Why don't you recognize the fact that you're finished. You and the other ranchers who try to fight me.'

'A pretty speech and the kind I expected from a killer like you,' called Cawdrey from the darkness. He seemed intent on keeping the other's attention focused on him, perhaps realizing that this might give Clem a chance to get within range of the rustlers. 'But you ain't convincin' anybody here. You've rustled too many head of cattle, killed too many men for us to allow you to get away this time. The tables have been turned and now you're forced into a corner. You've lost plenty of your men tonight and Haswell is no longer alive to send you any more information and betray us.'

'Haswell was no longer of any use to me. He'd outlived his usefulness.'

Carefully, Clem twisted himself around, crawled forward across the last two yards and moved into the hut. The door hung on rusted, broken hinges and the wooden floorboards gave ominously under his weight. Some were so rotten that they snapped as he crawled over them and it seemed impossible that those rustlers could fail to hear the noise. But he drew no shots from the tunnel and a moment later he was safely inside, crouched behind the open window that looked out on to the rocks.

This had evidently been a store place when the mines had been in production. He looked about him with more than a casual interest. There were tools stacked in one corner, shovels and picks and a couple of stout wooden boxes which lay against the far wall. He moved over to them, ducked instinctively as a smashing volley rang out from the darkness. A bullet tore its way through the flimsy wood of the wall and cracked across the hut over his head. Another ricocheted off the roof and he distinctly caught the wail of its flight.

But there was something about those boxes which seemed familiar. They had obviously been opened and then closed again in a hurry, as if someone had not wanted their contents to be discovered. Working quickly, he prised up the lid of the nearer box. It resisted his efforts for a moment, then sprang open as he put all of his strength into the attempt.

Inside, dimly seen, were several sticks of dynamite, already fused. The high explosive which had been used in the blasting of those tunnels out there, put here when they had been closed and forgotten ever since. He wondered briefly if Warburg and the rustlers knew that they were there. If he did, there was just the chance that he might try to use them against Cawdrey if the fight began to go against him.

Clem reached in and took half a dozen out of the box. Going back to the window, he peered out into the darkness. He could just see the faint muzzle flashes of the outlaws' guns in the dark tunnel less than twenty feet away, knew that several of them were crouched near the entrance, behind the boulders which had fallen there, providing then with excellent cover against the hail of lead which was being thrown at them from the other side of the plateau.

Immune to bullets, perhaps, he thought grimly, but not to high explosive. He took the box of sulphur matches from the pocket of his shirt, crouched down further so that the spurt of flame might not be seen, and lit the fuses of four of the sticks of explosive. There had been a faint doubt in his mind, doubt that the fuses might not burn after being stored for so long. But they spluttered and sparked as he touched the head of the match to them and without hesitation, hurled them with all the strength in his arm into the opening of the tunnel.

For perhaps five seconds nothing happened. The desultory firing continued. Then he heard the savage yells as the firing stopped. Another ten seconds, fifteen. Then the dull explosions came, thunderous echoes flapping around the rocks, the vivid glares of orange flame almost blinding him as they burst into being just inside the tunnel mouth. The sticks of dynamite exploded so closely together, that the explosions formed one continuous blur of sound which hurt the eardrums and sent a little tremor fluttering in the pit of his stomach.

For a moment both sides seemed stunned by what had happened. Then Clem moved out of the shattered door of the hut, yelled loudly. 'All right. Get them before they can recover!'

Vaguely he was aware that the dark shapes of Cawdrey's men were running forward. They had covered three-quarters of the distance to the tunnel before there was any return fire. Clem heard the vicious hornet-hum of slugs passing dangerously close to his head as he rushed forward. The sharp smell of burnt explosive and fume caught at the back of his nostrils as he sucked in a deep breath and for a moment, his eyes blurred with tears, so that he could scarcely see where he was going. He stumbled over one of the upthrusting metal rails, went down on one knee as he tried to steady himself and heard a slug whine through the air where his head had been a second earlier.

Swiftly, fighting down the pain that jarred through his leg, Clem twisted around on the ground, brought himself up on one elbow and tried to peer through the hazing swirl of smoke and dust that blotted out the tunnel entrance. He was dimly aware of a man who came staggering out, still clutching a rifle, one arm hanging limply by his side. As he saw him, the man tried to lift the Winchester with his good arm, to hold it steady against his chest and line it up on Clem's body. Smoothly, ignoring the pain in his body, Clem brought the Colt up, the front sight just above the man's chest, needing only the swift, instinctive snap of the wrist to line it up and squeeze the trigger in the same instant, to send death flaming across the dimness. But before he could press the trigger to loose off that shot, the man released his tight-fisted hold on the rifle. The long barrel tilted downward. Slowly, as though the muscles of his body were no longer able to obey the mental demands made on them – slow and reluctantly, the man sank forward on to his knees, hung there for a long moment, mouth working but with no sound coming out, then flopped on to his face and lay still.

A dry tongue, touching dry lips, Clem went forward, forcing one foot in front of the other. Inside the tunnel entrance everything was a shambles. Huge boulders had been split by the titanic force of the high explosive. Others had been brought down from the roof of the tunnel, although deeper in the hillside, the damage seemed confined to part of the rail system and one of the wagons, filled with ore and forgotten, now hurled over on to its side, the red stone spilling from it into a large pile.

A burst of firing came from deeper within the mine. A man, rushing forward beside Clem, suddenly uttered a - harsh shriek and fell forward, clutching at the torn chest, blood oozing between his clenched fingers. Behind them, Cawdrey's booming voice cried: 'Now we've got 'em on the run. Don't spare a single one. If you find Warburg, don't kill him. I want to see him die.'

Again that savage anger in the other's voice. Again Clem felt the sense of mystery. What was the connection between Warburg and Cawdrey? Certainly there seemed to be a very special link between these two. Something which had happened in the past and was now being brought to a head.

'You don't think you'll take me, do you, Cawdrey.' The harsh voice that Clem had heard before, throwing his challenge out to the rancher. It seemed to come from somewhere deeper inside the tunnel, among the broad wooden beams which had been hammered stoutly into place to keep up the roof.

'Better give yourself up while you have the chance,'

roared Cawdrey, his voice booming and echoing in the long emptiness of the tunnel. 'I'll see that you get a fair trial.'

'You don't expect me to believe that, do you. You'd shoot me down in cold blood the minute I stepped in front of your gun.' A burst of hard, derisive laughter, then a couple of shots that bucketed through the length of the tunnel. Out of the corner of his eye, Clem saw Cawdrey throw himself suddenly to one side as the slugs ricocheted along the tunnel from one side to the other. More firing broke out and it was evident that there were still several of the rustlers alive, still men ready and willing to continue the fight.

A couple of men rushed from behind a pile of wooden props, firing from the hip as they came. Clem swung to meet them, caught one full in the face with a bullet, saw the other go down in a tangled heap as one of the men beside him fired instinctively. Without pausing to think, heedless of the bullets that fled through the dank air inside the black tunnel, knowing that it was almost impossible to see more than a couple of yards in that darkness, Clem lifted himself to his full height and yelled at the other men to follow him. All the time that the fighting had been going on, a little thought had been nagging at the back of his mind, but it had persistently refused to come out into the open, so that he might recognize it for what it was. Now he knew. The horses that the rustlers had ridden into this place. Where were they now? Certainly they were not tethered outside and it would have been a foolish thing for them to do, leave their mounts where any attacker might get at them. No – they were inside the tunnel somewhere, further in those black stygian depths, where the retreating men could pick them up and ride out through another exit. He cursed himself for not having realized it before.

Everything seemed to be noise and confusion as he

fought his way forward, came upon Cawdrey crouched behind one of the trucks.

'We'd better try to rush 'em,' he said loudly, raising his voice to make himself heard above the racket of gunfire. 'They'll have their horses tucked away somewhere along the tunnel, ready to take off as soon as they realize they won't be able to hold us.'

He saw the tight expression on the rancher's face, saw the quick nod of understanding. Cawdrey yelled an order. The men came crowding forward on both sides of the tunnel. There was a clatter of feet on the rocks, a reverberation as the gunfire rose to an ear-shattering crescendo. Just how much was this roof going to stand before it came down about their ears? wondered Clem as he ran forward. He snapped two quick shots at a man who ran swiftly into the darkness, missed with both. Then the hammers clicked on empty chambers and he was forced to halt and reload from his belt.

The rustlers were pulling back now and the mere fact that they seemed quite prepared to do this rather than try to fight their way through Cawdrey's men, only served to strengthen Clem's belief that their mounts were somewhere to the rear and that once they reached them they would be able to ride out of the hills and there would be no chance of following them. With their own horses back at the entrance to the tunnel, there would not be time to return for them and ride after the survivors.

Running forward savagely, the guns in his hands pumping up and down as he fired shot after shot into the running, fleeting shadows, Clem kept close on the heels of the retreating men. But he was not close enough. Ahead of him, the darkness did not seem as absolute as before. It was still blackness, but there were faint gleams set in it and several seconds fled before he recognized the stars and realized that he was looking out at the open night sky.

Then, as if to confirm it for him, he felt the cold rush of air on his face, touching the flesh of his forehead where the sweat had worked its way through the open pores and lay on his skin. Men moved up behind him, surged out into the open.

There was a sudden movement less than fifty yards away. Clem swung round as he caught sight of it, sucked in his lips harshly and brought up the Colts, loosing off shot after shot as the men swung up into the saddles of the waiting horses, then wheeled and began to ride out of the narrow cutting between the rearing columns of rock. In the distance there was a sound that was familiar to every man there. The lowing of a herd of cattle.

Two men fell from their saddles as Clem fired, scarcely bothering to take aim. They crashed under the feet of the horses, did not move as the hoofs struck them and hammered them to the ground.

Running crouched over, he reached the rocks that looked out on to a wide clearing in the hills, whose presence he would never have suspected. There was part at least, of the herds which had been rustled. But he did not concern himself with this. Instead, he narrowed his eyes and tried to pick out the shapes of the riders moving away through the twisting trail that led downward into the clearing. He snapped more shots in their direction, heard a man let loose a loud yell, knew that he had hit him bad. But the clatter of hoofs on the bare rock still continued, the sound diminishing into the distance. He lowered the guns reluctantly. No sense in wasting any more lead shooting at shadows that were well out of range.

'Who got away?' Cawdrey came up, asked the question harshly, catching a tight grip on Clem's arm.

'I don't know. But I reckon one of them was Goudie, the man I want. The other man I couldn't see.'

Something came to Cawdrey's face in that instant. A

hardening of the muscles under the cheek and along the strong line of his jaw. The fingers which still held Clem's arm tightened convulsively until they bit deeply into the flesh. 'I'm sure it was Warburg. He's still alive. If he was dead, then we'd have found him back there.'

Clem turned. 'Warburg?'

'That's right. He was the leader of these rustlers, one of the most vicious killers in the territory. During the war, he rode with Quantrill, raiding and killing, pillaging and looting for the sheer delight of it. He rode into a town south of here where they went plundering and shooting. One of the people who was shot was my wife. When I heard of it, I swore I'd find her killer and mete out my own kind of justice. But it took me a long tune to discover the man who had done it, the man who had pulled the trigger. It wasn't Quantrill, although I suppose he ought to have been held morally responsible for her death at least. It was one of his lieutenants. A man called Justice Warburg.'

Clem nodded, understanding now the reason for the deep and lasting hatred in the other.

'I traced him halfway across the country after the war was over. It wasn't easy and there were times when I thought I'd lost him, that I'd never pick up his trail again. But I did. I had men looking for him, listening for any mention of his name. Whether or not he knew I was hunting him down, I don't know. I think in the end he must have suspected it. Then he turned rustler. It was something that came easy to him, I reckon.' Bitterness had crept into the other's voice. 'But when he came back into this territory, I knew it would be either him or me who would die.'

'So you've been waging this war against the rustlers, the Texas Dusters, not so much because they've been rustling your beef, but because of Warburg.'

'That's right.' Cawdrey nodded. 'Now it looks as if he's

slipped through my fingers again. He won't come back here into these hills. His power has been broken tonight. Nearly all of his men killed or scattered to the four winds. There's nothing to hold him here.'

'Maybe there is,' Clem gazed thoughtfully out into the dark night, out over the rocks to a horizon which he could not see.

'What do you mean?' Cawdrey looked up at him, his lips still tight. 'You think there is something that might make him remain?'

Clem grinned tightly. 'He's riding out there with Goudie. I'm sure of that and if I know Goudie, he won't leave empty-handed. They've been forced to leave this herd behind. They haven't had time to move it out and now it's lost to them.'

'You think they'll go for the bank in Bitter Ridge?'

'With Goudie, it will be either that or the stage.'

'There won't be a stage through Bitter Ridge for another four days. Even then it's unlikely they would get much from the kind of passengers who travel through this territory.'

'Then the answer seems fairly obvious. We'd better get back into town as quickly as we can if you want to settle your score with Warburg.'

They reached the edge of town shortly before dawn the next morning and circled into the main street in a tight bunch. In front of them the town seemed deceptively quiet; nothing moved on the street and only the howl of a dog that greeted the coming dawn, broke the silence for a few moments.

Clem sat tight in the saddle with Cawdrey beside him. The old rancher's face was etched deep with the lines of strain and Clem guessed that the happenings of the past night had taken their toll on him. The other was not as young a man as he thought himself to be, but he would hear none of the suggestions that he should ride back to the ranch and leave the fighting to the rest of the men.

As they sat there, silent, watchful, the door of one of the stores, right on the edge of town suddenly creaked open. So tensed was he, that Clem swung instantly at the sound, his right hand flashing for the gun at his belt. Then he forced himself to relax, to lower his hand as the old luau stepped out into the street, a broom in his hand, brushing away the dirt from the doorway. He glanced up, as if aware of them for the first time, and a startled look came into his eyes. For a moment, he hesitated, then turned as if to run back into the building.

'Hold it there, old-timer!' Clem called sharply.

The man stopped dead in his tracks and stood thoroughly still, as if expecting a bullet in the back. Evidently he had not recognized Cawdrey in the dim light and thought the men there might be outlaws.

Clem urged his mount forward until he stopped only a few feet from the old man. 'Anybody ridden into town in the last few hours?' he asked.

The other turned and stared up at him, screwing up his eyes as he tried to make out who it was sitting on the horse. 'Who're you?' he asked in a quavering, tremulous tone.

'My name would mean nothing to you,' said Clem sharply. 'But you probably recognize Mister Cawdrey there.' He gestured with his hand back towards the bunch of grim-faced men a few yards away at the very end of the street. The old man let his glance slide towards the riders, then he nodded.

'Sure, sure. What happened?'

'The world fell down as far as that gang of rustlers in the hills are concerned. They're either killed or scattered. But we know that two got away from us and we reckon they may have headed for town. If they did, then they'd have to

152

come this way. You seem like an early riser and a light sleeper. Did you hear anything?'

'There was a couple of riders came in about an hour ago. They seemed to be in an all-fired hurry.'

'Recognize either of 'em?'

'Nope.' The other shook his grizzled head emphatically. 'Never seen either of 'em before in my life. But they rode along the trail out there as if all the devils in hell were after 'em.' He chuckled. 'So that's what happened. I reckon there'll be a lot of rejoicing in the ranches around here when they hear of this night's work.'

'Mebbe so. But those two men were the most dangerous of them all. We have to find 'em before they start any more trouble. You got any idea where they might have gone, if they holed up here in town or not?'

'I heard 'em ride on into the middle of town, then the sound of their horses seemed to stop. It didn't die away as you'd expect it to if they'd ridden on through without stopping.'

'So you reckon they're still here in town?'

'I reckon so.'

Clem gave a tight nod as he wheeled his mount and went back to the others. It wasn't really much to go on. The old man could have been mistaken quite easily. Hearing was the most deceptive of the senses, especially during the stillness of the night when there were few other sounds.

Cawdrey stared at Clem's face. 'So they might still be here. Looks as though you could be right.' He turned to the men with him. 'You all heard that. Warburg and this killer Goudie may still be in town. Spread out and go after them.'

The men dismounted, tethered their mounts to the hitching rail in front of the store and slipped off into the shadows. Within moments, they had been swallowed up in the gloom that still lay over the town.

Cawdrey paused for a moment, sitting tall and straight in the saddle, as he looked about him, eyes growing accustomed to the gloom, picking out the shapes of the buildings on either side of the main street. It was still dark, and the faint light in the east did little more than suggest outlines for the majority of the buildings there. It wanted another hour or so to full daylight but there was enough light to see where the hotel stood head and shoulders above all of the other buildings in the town, halfway along the street. Beyond it, Clem remembered, on the opposite side of the street and perhaps fifty yards further on, stood the bank. If he had guessed right, that was where Goudie and Warburg might be at that moment, relying on them still being in the hills looking for them, too busy to come riding straight back to town.

As the silence continued, Clem felt the nerves in the pit of his stomach tighten into a hard knot. He knew from the other's face that the same thing was happening to Cawdrey and was not surprised when the man suddenly threw up the reins and slid from the saddle, leading the horse over to the hitching rail, wrapping the ends of the reins tightly around the wooden bar.

He glanced up towards Clem. 'You coming?' he asked softly. There was an odd tightness in his voice, as if he did not trust himself to speak evenly, and was talking with an effort.

Clem paused, then nodded, stepped down and tethered his mount. He eased the sixers in their holsters as he fell in beside the other and together, in full view of anyone who might be watching, unlike the other men who were at that moment scattered throughout the town, they walked along the middle of the dusty street.

There was no sign of horses in the street, Clem noticed. He had half-expected to see the two mounts tethered somewhere in the vicinity of the bank, knowing that neither of the two men were fools and they would have their horses somewhere close by ready for a quick getaway if it proved necessary.

It was only a momentary thought. Deep in the thundering rush of feeling that came with the knowledge that Goudie should not be very far away, the chill of his anger came in a cold counter-current. Fighting for control, he felt the anger slip away, tightened the mental grip on himself, and moved his gaze slowly from one side of the street to the other, watchful for the slightest movement along the shadowed boardwalks, or in the darkness that still lurked in the doorways.

Now the brick building of the bank stood less than fifty yards away. It stood silent and apparently deserted. Not a single light showed in any of the windows, and there was not the slightest sound of movement there to indicate that either of the two men they were hunting was anywhere inside.

Clem paused, caught at the other's arm. He gestured towards the boardwalk on the opposite side of the street to the bank. 'You get down there and keep an eye on the street door,' he said quietly. 'I'll work my way around to the back. Some of your men should be moving up soon and they may try to slip out once the shooting starts.'

'If they're inside,' whispered the other. He sounded dubious. 'Don't you think we ought to warn the sheriff?'

'He'll come running the minute we open fire,' Clem told him. 'Make no mistake about that.'

'Still it might be best if he was to know. He may think that—' The other broke off. Across the street, the door of the bank had suddenly opened and a dark figure stepped out on to the wooden boardwalk. Swiftly, Clem jerked his guns from their holsters.

'Hold it there,' he called loudly.

The man was a grey and not wholly distinct shadow in the doorway. Even before the warning was out of Clem's mouth, he had leapt back with a sudden shout and a shot flamed from the window of the bank as the other man, inside, opened up on them. The bullet hit the street a yard from the two men, raised a spurt of dust. For a moment, Cawdrey stood stock still, shocked by the suddenness with which things had happened. Grabbing him with one hand, Clem hauled him back across the street, pushed him down behind the horse trough which stood on the side. A bullet struck the top of it and whined into the distance, smashing into the woodwork behind them.

'Keep your head down unless you want to get it blown off,' he hissed harshly. 'They mean business.'

Clem moved steadily sideways, keeping one eye on the building across the street. He could see no movement there now and the street door had been slammed shut. Then, abruptly, the window beside the door was shattered into a hundred pieces as a revolver barrel struck it. Two more shots hammered across the street. Clem heard the slugs thud into the woodwork of the boardwalk behind him as he slithered forward. They sounded close but he did not pause to find out. Reaching the end of the board-walk, where it dipped down on to the street, as an alley opened out on to it, he got his legs under him, waited for a moment, then thrust himself forward, using all of the strength in his legs to propel himself across the alley and into the shadows on the other side.

The move took the men inside the bank by surprise and by the time they opened tip on him again, trying to seek him out, he had moved further around and was too wide of the bank for their guns to reach him.

He listened to the sound of shooting carefully as he paused there, then moved across to the other side of the street, edged forward along the boardwalk, treading carefully, making no noise. They would be expecting him, would be waiting for him, but that was a chance he had to take. He knew the kind of man that Goudie was, a born killer, a vicious murderer and a very cunning man. About Warburg, he knew nothing apart from what Cawdrey had told him, but he sounded like a man tarred with the same brush.

More gunfire sounded as he drew close to the bank. Further along the street he saw three men advancing swiftly at a run, recognized them as more of Cawdrey's men and relaxed. Very soon the two men inside the bank would realize they were surrounded, that there was no chance for them to escape and then it would be up to them whether they surrendered or fought it out to the end. Inwardly, he felt certain they would fight it out, knowing what lay in store for them if they were taken prisoner.

'What the hell's going on here?'

Sheriff Howell's voice calling along the street. Clem saw him running forward out of the shadows. He paused as a shot from the bank whistled close to him, then dived for cover. Clem saw him wriggling forward until he was with Cawdrey.

'Better stay where you are, Sheriff.' Goudie shouted the warning from the window. 'Anybody comes any closer and we'll shoot him down.'

'You can't get away with this,' yelled Howell. 'Throw down your guns and come out.'

A harsh laugh from one of the men in the bank. Then Warburg shouted. 'We mean to walk out of here and ride out of town, Sheriff, and if you try to stop us, Maclean here is going to get a bullet in his back.'

Clem stopped, hugged the wall a few feet from the window. He recalled Maclean, the little bank manager. Somehow, this pair must have got hold of him and were holding him as a hostage there. He sucked in his breath.

That complicated matters.

'You in there, Maclean?' called Howell.

A pause, then a man's quavering voice called: 'Yes, I'm here, Sheriff. For God's sake do as they say. They mean to shoot me down if you don't.'

'Your move, Sheriff,' called Warburg harshly.

Edging back, Clem moved into the narrow alley beside the bank, circling the building. There were no more shots fired in the main street. Evidently Sheriff Howell was taking Warburg's threat seriously. There was a small window half-way along that side of the building. He took a chance, hit it squarely with the butt of his gun. The glass smashed inward. He heard a sudden yelling from the street; guessed that more of Cawdrey's men had arrived on the scene.

Without pausing, he wriggled through the window, found himself in a small room at the end of a long corridor. It was a store room of some kind and he pushed his way across it as quickly as he could. Out in the corridor, which he guessed led to the front of the building, he looked to right and left, discovered nothing, but he knew that there had to be a door leading into the main section of the bank. Another three steps and his outstretched hand encountered the door. He touched the knob, felt it turn under his fingers.

For a long moment, he paused there. Beyond the door he could hear the murmur of voices as the two men talked between themselves. Sucking in a long gust of air, he let it come out from between his lips in slow pinches, making scarcely any sound. One wrong move on his part, one moment of hesitation when he stepped through into that room behind the others and the bank manager would be the first to die. He knew instinctively that neither of the two men in there would hesitate to draw on the helpless man and shoot him down in cold blood.

Gripping the Colt tightly in his right hand, he caught hold of the doorknob in his left and twisted it quickly. It made a slight squeal of sound. Then he jerked the door open, stepped through, focusing his gaze on the two men who stood behind the windows. The small figure of the bank manager stood a few feet away. Clem wanted to yell to him in that instant, to call to him to drop flat on his face, but he knew that the warning, even if he gave it, would be seconds too late. Already, Goudie was swinging round, bringing his gun to bear. There was a thin sneer on his face as he recognized Clem, standing there in the doorway.

'I shot your partner, and I'll finish the job with you,' he grated harshly. Swiftly, he brought the barrel of his gun to bear, his finger tightening on the trigger. Before he could fire, Clem's gun bucked in his hand. The burned powder blossomed red-crimson in the darkness of the room. Goudie staggered as the bullet took him in the chest. He tried desperately to hold life in his body, to force his arm to rise. It came up reluctantly, then dropped as Clem fired again.

As he fell, Clem swung to cover Warburg, but the other had moved swiftly, not going for his gun as Clem had expected, but across the room, stepping behind the small figure of the bank manager, catching him tightly around the waist, holding him as a shield. His gun came up, as Clem moved swiftly back, crouching against the wall.

'If you try to shoot me, you'll hit the old man,' snarled the other harshly.

Clem stood there helplessly. What the other said was true. He could not risk getting off a shot at Warburg while he held the older man in front of him as a shield. He was forced to watch as Warburg moved back towards the door, still retaining his hold on the man. Still holding the gun, the other reached behind him and opened the door

159

slightly. Raising his voice, he called: 'You there, outside. I'm coming out and I've got Maclean with me. Any wrong move by any of you and he gets it first. Understand?'

There was silence out in the street. Through the smashed window, Clem could see that the dawn was greying the street. Warburg opened the door wider and took a step backwards, dragging the unresisting man with him.

There was only one chance and Clem took it. Stepping away from the wall, exposing himself to the other's fire, he lifted the gun, moving forward.

'So you want to die, ranger.' The other brought up his gun, levelled it at Clem. A second later, a shot rang out. Clem braced himself involuntarily, then saw the gunman in the doorway buckling at the knees. The gun slipped from his fingers and fell to the floor. A look of stupefied amazement spread over his face. Then the muscles loosened and he dropped forward, his head striking against Maclean's legs, throwing him off-balance.

Cawdrey came into the room a few moments later, the smoking gun still clutched in his hand. He stood for a long moment, staring down at the dead man on the floor, then looked up at Clem.

'I finally got my revenge,' he said in a tight, throaty voice. 'I'm only sorry that I had to shoot him in the back. It was the only way.'

Clem grinned tightly. 'You'll never know how much I was relying on you to do that,' he said thinly. He glanced across at the sheriff. 'I reckon you'll find that this has smashed the entire rustling outfit, Sheriff.'

Leaving the bank, he walked out into the grey dawn, stood for a moment, then made his way towards the hotel where Doc Foran would undoubtedly be waiting for him.